DEADLY FAMILY SECRETS

K.D. RICHARDS

INTRIGUE

Recycling programs for this product may not exist in your area.

ISBN-13: 978-1-335-18909-7

Deadly Family Secrets

Harlequin Enterprises ULC
22 Adelaide St. West, 41st Floor
Toronto, Ontario M5H 4E3, Canada
www.Harlequin.com

HarperCollins Publishers
Macken House, 39/40 Mayor Street Upper,
Dublin 1, D01 C9W8, Ireland
www.HarperCollins.com

Printed in Lithuania

1 2 3 4 5 6 7 8 9 10 LIT 28 27 26 25

The crack of the gunshot split the silence.

Tyson was moving, years of training taking over in an instant. “Get down!” he shouted, launching himself toward Olivia. He collided with her, one arm wrapping around her waist as he tackled her to the ground behind her car.

“Are you hit?” he asked, running his hands over her arms, her sides, checking for blood or injury.

“No,” she managed, her voice tight with fear but steady enough to reassure him. “No, I’m okay.”

More shots rang out.

“Stay down,” he ordered, his voice low and urgent against her ear as he covered her body with his own. He listened carefully, trying to pinpoint the direction they were coming from.

The shooting had stopped. Tyson strained his ears, listening for movement, for any indication of what the shooter might be doing. Had they fled? Or were they just repositioning?

“I think they’re moving,” he whispered to Olivia, who was pressed against him, her body trembling but her eyes clear and focused. “I need to go after them.”

Her fingers dug into his arm. “Tyson—”

“I can’t let them get away.”

K.D. Richards is a native of the Washington, DC, area, who now lives outside Toronto with her husband and two sons. You can find her at kdrichardsbooks.com.

Books by K.D. Richards

Harlequin Intrigue

Guardians of Justice

Killer on the Potomac
Death by Data
Cold Case Cover-Up
Deadly Family Secrets

West Investigations

Pursuit of the Truth
Missing at Christmas
Christmas Data Breach
Shielding Her Son
Dark Water Disappearance
Catching the Carling Lake Killer
Under the Cover of Darkness
A Stalker's Prey
Silenced Witness
Lakeside Secrets
Under Lock and Key
The Perfect Murder

Visit the Author Profile page at Harlequin.com.

CAST OF CHARACTERS

Olivia Lowell—Graphic designer in search of her birth family.

Tyson Morrow—Chief of police in Galesburg.

Annalise Farr—Olivia's birth mother (deceased).

Ameila Farr—Olivia's aunt and Annalise's sister.

Stephanie Santini—Amelia's daughter and Olivia's cousin.

Chapter One

Olivia Lowell stood frozen on the sidewalk across from Amelia's Café, her throat dry despite the humidity of the Delaware summer afternoon. Through the large front windows, she could see patrons inside eating and drinking. Going about their day oblivious to the fact that for her, walking into the café could possibly be a life-changing act.

"Just walk across the street," she whispered to herself, clutching the weathered birth certificate in her purse as if it were a talisman. "And go in. Don't lose your nerve now."

Her reflection in a parked car's window caught her attention. Her light brown curls framed her oval face, and her hazel eyes were wide with nervousness. Nothing like her mother's thin face and dark brown hair that would never hold a curl. That was okay. She'd always known she was adopted, and she couldn't have wished for a better mother than Lattice Lowell, but there was always a part of her that wanted to know about her birth parents. For thirty-five years, it had been just the two of them. But now she was alone, her mother having suddenly been taken by a heart attack far too soon. Well, almost alone. While she was alive, her mother had been adamant that there was no way to know who Olivia's birth mother was, and she hadn't pressed the issue. But as she'd sorted through her mother's belongings after her death, the grief still raw, she discovered her original birth certificate tucked inside an old photo album. “Annalise Farr.” Her birth mother’s name.

Her anger at her mother for the deception had only been tempered by the possibility that she might have family, might not be so utterly alone, after all.

A horn blared, startling her. She took a deep breath, inhaling the sweet scent wafting from the café across the street.

“Just go in,” she murmured, staring at the green cursive sign that read Amelia’s Café.

The private investigator she’d hired had found Annalise Farr. Unfortunately, all the hopes she may have had for a happy mother-daughter reunion were dashed a moment later when the PI informed her that Annalise had been killed not long after putting her infant daughter up for adoption in a hit-and-run accident. Now Olivia grieved for two mothers, but she’d also found an aunt and a cousin. Annalise’s sister, Amelia, and Amelia’s daughter, Stephanie. It was hard to believe they’d lived less than a two-hour drive away for her entire life.

A couple exited the café, the woman laughing at something her companion said. Before she could talk herself out of it, Olivia stepped off the curb and dashed across the street, catching the door before it swung all the way closed.

No one looked up as she entered. Most of the patrons appeared engrossed in conversation or bent over laptops.

The café itself was warm and inviting. The walls were painted yellow, the artwork depicted various lakeside scenes, and soft rock music came from the overhead speakers. The scent of coffee, sugar and baking pastries wrapped around the space.

She approached the counter. A woman in her early thirties was taking an order from a tall man in a well-cut charcoal suit. The woman wore a canvas apron with “Amelia’s” emblazoned across the chest in the same green cursive as the sign outside. Her hair was piled in a neat bun atop her head, and her caramel-colored skin glowed under the pendant lights.

The woman smiled at the customer as she handed him his receipt. Olivia's breath caught. The private investigator had been able to find a single old photograph of Annalise online. Looking at the woman behind the counter was like looking at that old photograph of her birth mother—the same high cheekbones, the same full lips, the same dimple in the left cheek.

No, she realized with a jolt. *Not just like Annalise. Like me too.*

She gripped the counter to steady herself. The nameplate on the woman's apron gave her name as Stephanie. This had to be her cousin Stephanie. She finished with her customer and turned toward Olivia, her smile professional and warm.

Olivia's legs trembled. She could still leave. Walk out the door, drive home to DC and pretend she'd never found that birth certificate. Her mother's voice echoed in her mind. *We're all the family we need, Olivia.*

But Olivia wasn't sure she believed that or had ever believed that. And her mother wasn't here anymore.

She walked to the counter.

"Welcome to Amelia's. What can I get for you?" Stephanie said with the familiar pleasant lilt used by many a barista. A moment later, she tilted her head, her posture subtly shifting as her eyes lingered on Olivia's face. Recognition, or more likely confusion, flickered over her face.

Olivia's mouth went dry. "I'm… I'm not really here for coffee," she said. "Is Amelia here? I'd… I'd like to speak to her."

Stephanie's expression changed; her green eyes, at least there was one difference between them, narrowed with suspicion.

"I'm sorry. Who are you? And how do you know my mother?" The warmth had evaporated from Stephanie's voice.

The swinging door behind the counter pushed open before Olivia could formulate an answer. An older woman bustled out, carrying a tray of pastries. Her silver-streaked hair was piled atop her head in the same style as Stephanie's, and though time had etched lines around her eyes and mouth, there was no denying the family resemblance.

"These are fresh from the oven. Cherry…" the woman, Amelia, said, her voice trailing off as her gaze locked with Olivia's. All the color drained from her face in an instant. The tray slipped from her fingers, clattering to the floor as tarts scattered across the polished wood.

"Mom! Are you okay?" Stephanie moved quickly, grasping her mother's arm and guiding her from behind the counter to a nearby table. She eased her into a chair, concern etched across her features. "Sit here, Mom. I'll get you some water." Then, noticing that the commotion had silenced the café, she forced a smile onto her face and said, "Nothing to worry about. Just a little mishap."

For a moment, the café remained quiet before conversation cautiously resumed.

Throughout it all, Amelia's gaze hadn't wavered from Olivia's face. The woman sat rigidly in the chair, looking as if she'd seen a ghost.

As Stephanie hurried back behind the counter, Olivia approached Amelia's table. Her pulse hammered so violently she feared it might burst from her chest. The older woman's eyes, the same green as her daughter's, followed her every movement.

"Amelia," Olivia said, her voice trembling, "my name is Olivia Lowell. I… I don't know how to say this, but I think you're my aunt."

For a moment, Amelia's expression softened. But then her face hardened. She shook her head firmly. "No. I'm sorry, but

I'm not your aunt. I'm not." The words came out sharp, brittle. "You need to go."

Olivia staggered back as if she'd been physically struck. She'd tried to prepare herself for every possible reaction but wasn't sure she could have prepared for how much Amelia's outright rejection hurt. The woman wasn't even giving her a chance to explain who she was and why she believed they were related.

Amelia's voice grew stronger, more certain. "Go. Now. And please don't come back."

The café suddenly became too warm, too crowded. Olivia could feel the curious glances of nearby patrons even as they pretended not to be listening. Stephanie returned with a glass of water, confusion clear on her face as she looked between her mother and the stranger who so eerily resembled them.

"Mom, what—" Stephanie began.

"Everything's fine," Amelia said, cutting her off, still staring at Olivia. "This young woman was just leaving."

Something fierce and protective flashed in Amelia's eyes. Not hatred, Olivia realized with sudden clarity, more like fear. Whatever secrets lay in their shared past, Amelia wanted to leave them buried there.

Olivia fumbled in her purse, drawing out her folded birth certificate and placing it on the table. "I found this after my mother died," she said quietly. "Lattice Lowell adopted me thirty-five years ago. But my birth mother was Annalise Farr. Your sister."

Stephanie gasped, her gaze darting between her mother and Olivia.

Amelia didn't touch the document. Her hands remained clasped tightly in her lap, knuckles white. "I asked you to leave," she said, voice lower, almost pleading.

Amelia wouldn't meet her gaze now. That alone told Olivia

everything she needed to know. Annalise Farr was her mother and Amelia Farr was her aunt. An aunt who didn't want to know her. Her heart broke into thousands of pieces, but she'd spent enough years masking her feelings that it was easy not to let it show. Not to these people who may have been related by blood but would never be her family.

She slid her birth certificate back into her purse.

"I'm sorry to have upset you." She stepped away from the table, keeping her head held high as she walked back to the café's entrance. The space that had seemed so welcoming moments earlier now felt suffocating.

TYSON MORROW PULLED his police cruiser into the circular driveway of the lake house, gravel crunching beneath the tires. He cut the engine and sat, taking in the view. Dusk was settling over the mountains, the sun's dying rays painting the sky in vivid strokes of orange and pink. Light sparkled across the lake's surface. As beautiful as ever, he thought, allowing himself a brief appreciation of the scene. He'd seen this same view captured in countless paintings displayed around town, but no artist had truly done it justice. Nothing compared to the real thing, and it never grew old.

His moment of serenity evaporated as his gaze shifted to the A-frame glass lake house in front of him. Irritation prickled. These lakeside mansions represented everything that got under his skin about the tourists who visited their town. They loved to put their ostentatious wealth on display along with their casual disrespect for the locals.

"This is what you signed up for when you took the job of chief and moved from LA," he reminded himself under his breath. He sighed heavily and stepped out of the police cruiser.

The evening air was cool and fresh with the scent of pine and fresh water. His heart lightened at the smell. At least being chief of police in Galesburg meant being home again, surrounded by the people who had known him before he'd left, first to join the military and after his discharge to join the police force in Los Angeles. He'd been back in Galesburg for a year. A year that had been somewhat of an adjustment, but the old rhythms of a small-town life were becoming comfortable again, like a well-worn sweatshirt.

He climbed the steps of the front porch, his boots heavy on the polished wood and pressed the doorbell, hearing an elaborate melodic chime echo through the house. He allowed himself a quick eye roll at the sound then squared his shoulders, preparing for whatever entitled summer resident might answer.

After several moments, one side of the double doors swung open, and he was caught off guard by the woman standing on the threshold. She was striking. Beautiful dark skin, remarkable hazel eyes that caught the fading light, and a cascade of curly hair falling past her shoulders.

Collecting himself quickly, he said, "Ma'am, I'm Tyson Morrow, Galesburg chief of police. Are you Olivia Lowell?"

"Yes," she answered, her voice carrying a hint of wariness.

"May I come in?" he asked, maintaining his professional demeanor.

Indecision crossed her face before she moved back, wordlessly allowing him to step inside.

The foyer was exactly what he'd expected, ostentatious wealth on display. Marble floors gleamed beneath his feet, and an actual crystal chandelier hung overhead. What he could see of the living and dining rooms suggested furniture that likely cost more than his entire modest home. A curved staircase led to the upper level, and he could see clear through to the rear of the house, which boasted a spectacular view of the lake and mountains through a wall of window.

His jaw tightened. The display only aggravated his already simmering annoyance.

"Can I get you a glass of water, Chief?" Olivia asked, breaking into his thoughts.

"No," Tyson replied, the word coming out harsher than he'd intended.

Surprise flashed in her eyes at his tone. She took a step back, crossing her arms defensively over her chest.

"Then how can I help you?" she asked, her voice taking on a chill that he immediately categorized as snooty entitlement.

"Were you at Amelia's Café earlier today?" he asked pointedly.

Her eyes narrowed suspiciously. "Yes."

"What was your business there?"

Her posture stiffened, spine going rigid. "I don't see how that is any of your business."

"Stephanie and Amelia Farr are pillars of this community," he said, feeling heat rise in his voice. "When I get word that someone has made trouble for them, I make it my business to put a stop to it."

Olivia scoffed, dropping her arms to her sides. "I did not make trouble for anyone."

"That's not what I heard," he countered, his patience wearing thin.

She took a step forward, challenging him. "Heard from who? Did Amelia say I caused trouble?"

"No," Tyson admitted through gritted teeth.

Amelia hadn't told him anything, but Galesburg operated on its own particular frequency. When a woman who looked enough like Amelia to be Stephanie's twin walked into the café, people noticed. They also noticed when that woman's sudden appearance nearly caused Amelia to pass out. He'd tried to get answers from Amelia herself, but she had been as tight-lipped as the woman standing before him.

Silence stretched between them, a battle of wills. But even as his annoyance spiked at the stubborn set of her jaw, he reluctantly acknowledged the unwanted attraction the flash of ire in her eyes sent through him. It was a combination that could bring a man to his knees.

Another man, he corrected himself firmly. He was there on…well, not quite official business, but he was definitely not there to ogle Olivia Lowell.

"I think you should leave, Chief Morrow," Olivia said, breaking the stalemate.

He remained rooted in place. "Are you planning to stay in town long, Ms. Lowell?"

"Miss," she said pointedly. "And once again, that's none of your business, Chief."

She strode to the door and pulled it open, standing beside it in clear dismissal. He moved slowly toward the door, pausing before crossing the threshold.

"Try to keep out of trouble, Miss Lowell," he said, unable to resist the parting shot.

Her jaw clenched visibly before she widened the door farther. "Good night, Chief," she replied through gritted teeth.

Chapter Two

Olivia sank deeper into the sofa's plush cushions, her fingers wrapped around a half-empty wineglass. On the television screen, characters moved through their drama, their voices nothing more than background noise to her churning thoughts. She took another sip, letting the rich cabernet linger on her tongue, but even the wine's warmth couldn't soothe her irritation. Chief Tyson Morrow's face appeared in her mind, that square jaw, those piercing eyes, the way his uniform hugged his broad shoulders. Devastatingly handsome, yes. But also insufferably arrogant.

She swirled the wine in her glass, still stewing an hour after he'd driven away. Who did he think he was, lecturing her about upsetting Amelia? He'd said her aunt hadn't sent him, but she wasn't sure she believed him. Maybe he just didn't want to make Amelia look like the bad guy.

The thought that Amelia had sicced the police on her stung more than she expected. She'd imagined many versions of this reunion, tears, embraces, maybe some initial awkwardness and suspicion, but not outright rejection. She had her original birth certificate after all. It was undeniable. She was Annalise Farr's daughter. But that wasn't enough for her Aunt Amelia.

But what if there was more to the story? She couldn't help recalling the flash of fear she'd seen in Amelia's eyes. Was her aunt afraid of her? Or for her? And why?

She let out a deep sigh. “Maybe it’s best to just accept that Amelia does not want you in her life and move on,” she whispered to herself, placing her glass on the coffee table with a decisive clink.

She had a good life in DC. Friends. She was a well-respected graphic designer with a thriving business. There was no lack of politicians or wanna-be celebrities wanting to “write” their memoir or pen a book on some subject or the other that they were supposedly an “expert” in. The explosion of social media stars had opened up a stream of influencer-clients that had left her very comfortable financially speaking. She didn’t need Amelia Farr.

She would pack tonight and leave first thing in the morning. Return to her orderly life in DC and forget her foolish quest for family connections. She pushed herself up from the sofa and was halfway to standing when the doorbell’s unexpected chime froze her in place.

Her eyes darted to the ornate clock on the mantelpiece. Half past eight. A little late for visitors, but she was pretty sure she knew who waited on the other side of that door.

“Chief Morrow,” she hissed, heat rising in her cheeks. “Probably come to make sure I’m scurrying back to DC like a good little outsider.”

She marched to the door, each step fueled by indignation, ready to tell the handsome chief exactly what she thought of his meddling. She yanked the door open, a cutting remark poised on her lips, but it wasn’t Tyson Morrow’s towering frame that stared back at her.

“Hi,” Stephanie said, her smile faltering under Olivia’s startled gaze.

“Hi,” Olivia said, stunned.

“I’m sorry to come over unannounced, but do you mind if we talk?”

Olivia hesitated, her mind racing with suspicion. Was this some kind of trap? Amelia had made her feelings clear enough. Yet there was a genuineness in Stephanie's eyes that made her step aside.

"I was just having a glass of wine," she said. "Would you like one?"

Stephanie's face brightened immediately. "Yes, please."

Olivia led her unexpected guest to the living room and gestured toward the sofa where she'd been sitting before going into the kitchen. She took a moment to gather her wits before returning to the living room with a clean glass. She poured a glass and handed it to Stephanie before sitting on the opposite end of the sofa.

They took a few cautious sips of wine while studying the other silently over the rims of their glasses.

"This is really good," Stephanie said, holding her glass up to the light. A laugh escaped her. "Of course, I'd probably think anything was good right now. I have a fourteen-month-old at home who I just weaned. This is my first glass of wine in two years."

The admission softened something in Olivia's chest. She gave Stephanie a genuine smile. "Well, I'm glad I sprung for the good stuff then."

They clinked their glasses in a toast before taking another sip. Then Stephanie set her wine aside and turned to face Olivia directly, her expression growing serious. "I guess you're wondering why I'm here."

"I could say the same thing to you," Olivia countered, still not entirely ready to trust.

"Touché." Stephanie laughed before sobering again. "I'm here because I heard what you said to my mother. That you think she is your aunt."

Olivia's shoulders tensed. "Yes, I'm quite sure of it actually."

"Well, you look enough like Mom and me to be related. But how?"

Olivia set her wineglass down. "I was adopted soon after I was born. I've always known I was adopted, but my mother told me she didn't know who my birth mother was. I accepted that because I trusted her and it never really seemed important to know the woman who gave me up." She took a deep breath, girding herself for what came next. "My mother passed away six months ago from cancer."

Stephanie reached across the expanse of the sofa and took Olivia's hand, her face softening with sympathy. "I'm sorry for your loss."

"Thank you."

"While I was clearing out my mother's things, I found my original birth certificate. My birth mother's name is Annalise Farr."

"Aunt Annalise," Stephanie said.

Olivia nodded. "My mother. Your aunt. Which makes your mother—"

"Your aunt," Stephanie finished.

"Exactly."

Silence settled between them, heavy with unspoken questions. Olivia watched Stephanie's face closely, noting the confusion that confirmed what she'd suspected after the confrontation at the café. Stephanie hadn't known she existed.

That knowledge brought conflicting emotions. Relief that she wasn't the only one who'd been kept in the dark, but also a sharp, twisting pain that her birth mother and aunt had so thoroughly erased her from their lives.

"My mother never mentioned Aunt Annalise having a child," Stephanie said.

"I gathered that." Olivia reached for her wineglass and took another sip, hoping to wash away the bitterness in her tone. The warmth from the wine did nothing to ease the chill of rejection.

Stephanie reached for her wineglass again, taking a longer drink before asking, "I don't know why my mother reacted the way she did. Do you?"

"No," Olivia answered tersely.

Stephanie rolled her glass between her palms, thoughtful. "My mom obviously knew about you."

"You think so?" A part of her still clung to the hope that Amelia's reaction had been born of shock, not recognition.

"Definitely." Stephanie nodded emphatically. "She recognized you immediately. I mean, you do look a lot like us, and you're the spitting image of Aunt Annalise, at least the pictures I've seen of her. She died right before I was born."

"Do you mind if I ask how old you are?"

"I'm thirty-five," Olivia replied.

It would have been easy then, to keep her existence from Stephanie. "I'm a year older than you."

Stephanie drained her glass in one swift motion and set it firmly on the table. "I don't know what my mother knows or doesn't know, but we are going to find out."

The unexpected "we" caught Olivia off guard. "We? You believe me? That Annalise was my birth mother and you are my cousin?"

Stephanie cocked her head, studying Olivia with direct intensity. "Why shouldn't I believe you? Are you lying?"

A smile tugged at Olivia's lips despite herself. Her cousin's forthright manner couldn't be more different from her own careful restraint, but there was something endearing about it.

"No, I'm not lying. I believe the birth certificate is correct and Annalise Farr gave birth to me," she said. "But I do think we should do a DNA test to confirm it. I purchased a couple of kits online and brought them with me in case you agreed. It would be best if your mother and I took the test, but they can make a familial match between you and me."

Stephanie rose to her feet with sudden decisiveness. "Well, if you need my blood, you've got it. I have to go. Geo, my husband, and Hayes, my son, have been home alone all day, so who knows what I'll be walking into."

Olivia followed her to the front door, watching as Stephanie paused in the foyer and turned back.

"Come to Amelia's in the morning," Stephanie said. "We can have breakfast and you can talk to my mom."

Olivia's stomach twisted at the thought. "I don't think your mother would like that. She sent Chief Morrow to warn me away from Amelia's."

"No, she didn't." Stephanie shook her head firmly. "I mean, Tyson did come by the café to make sure Mom was okay after he heard you'd come in."

Something must have flashed across Olivia's face, because Stephanie continued quickly, "You have to understand, in a small town, word travels fast. My mom had a mild heart attack last year, and she is like a second mother to Tyson. He'd do anything for her. But she didn't ask him to talk to you. She barely uttered a word to him, or me, since she saw you."

The knot in Olivia's chest loosened. "Is your mother okay? I didn't mean to endanger her health."

Stephanie waved away the concern. "She's fine. I think you just surprised her."

"Surprised to see me," Olivia said, "but not that I existed."

Stephanie reached out and squeezed Olivia's hand gently. "Come to Amelia's tomorrow. Breakfast is on me. We'll talk, figure this out and get to know each other."

Olivia hesitated, weighing her options. This was what she

had come for, to discover her roots, to understand the family that had given her up. And Stephanie was offering a pathway to that knowledge even if her aunt wasn't along for the ride yet.

She nodded slowly. "I'll be there."

Chapter Three

The scotch burned in his throat, but it did nothing to steady his hands. He set the glass down on his desk with a tremor that sent amber liquid sloshing against crystal. His home office, usually his sanctuary, felt suffocating tonight. The familiar weight of mahogany furniture and leather-bound books pressed in around him.

Fear crawled beneath his skin. His life was unraveling. His secretary had been all too eager to share the gossip from the café, recounting Olivia's confrontation with Amelia Farr. The woman was an unabashed gossipmonger, spreading whatever little tidbits she came across through Galesburg as if it were her one true calling. But for once, he was glad she was a blabbermouth.

Annalise's baby. The thought struck him with the force of a physical blow. *His child.*

No. He caught himself, his jaw clenching. He couldn't think that way. Not ever. No one could know. No one could ever discover that he had fathered a child with Annalise. That secret had to remain buried, no matter the cost.

But it was her. Olivia. His and Annalise's daughter. He was certain of it now. He'd taken a foolish risk, taking his boat out onto the lake, but he'd had to see for himself. And he'd seen her on the back porch of her rental house with a glass of wine. The resemblance was unmistakable. She looked just like Annalise had, the same delicate features, the same way of holding herself.

His heart clenched at the memory. The mere thought of Annalise could resurrect feelings from thirty years ago. Annalise was his soulmate. He believed that then and now, despite everything that had happened between them. If circumstances had been different…

But it wasn't and he'd done what he had to do.

Now, after decades of carefully constructed safety, Olivia's presence threatened to tear down everything he'd built. She was asking questions, digging into the past with the same determination that had once made her mother so dangerous. He wouldn't, couldn't, let it happen.

Perhaps Olivia would prove more reasonable than Annalise had been. Perhaps he could frighten her away, back to Washington, DC, where he'd heard she lived. He would try, for Annalise's sake as much as his own.

But if Olivia proved to be as stubborn as her mother, if she refused to heed his warnings and continued her relentless pursuit of the truth…well, then he'd have no other choice.

He'd done what was necessary once before to protect his secrets.

And he would do it again if he had to.

Chapter Four

Olivia woke with a start, the early morning light filtering through unfamiliar curtains. She'd only fallen asleep a few hours earlier, too anxious about her impending breakfast at Amelia's Café to drift off. Her stomach knotted at the thought of facing her aunt again. Yesterday's reception was chilly enough to leave frost burns. But Stephanie had seemed genuine in her interest and desire to get to know her.

Pushing aside her apprehension, she dressed carefully in a soft blue shirt and skirt, hoping to make a good impression on her newfound family. Maybe Amelia had just been shocked. Maybe today would be different.

She gathered her courage and her purse, headed for the front door. She pulled it open and the sight in front of her stole her breath.

Bold, jagged letters sprawled across the handsome double doors in black spray paint. GO HOME.

The paint had dried, but it hadn't been there when Stephanie had left sometime after 9:00 p.m. But it was there now, screaming its hostility in the morning light.

Her hands trembled as she stepped back, bile rising in her throat. She pulled her phone from her pocket with shaking fingers and called the police. She waited on the porch for them to arrive, careful not to touch the door, her mind racing.

Who could have done this? No matter what her reaction had

been to Olivia's showing up the day before, she couldn't imagine her Aunt Amelia sneaking through the woods in the dark of night to vandalize the front door. The thought was absurd. And Stephanie had seemed genuinely welcoming, eager even, to get to know her. That could have been an act but to what end? Chief Morrow had mentioned that Amelia was a pillar of the community. Was it possible that someone who'd heard about Amelia's reaction to her presence had done this, thinking they were protecting her? The idea seemed unlikely, but what did she really know about Galesburg and its residents? Nothing, but so far, she wasn't impressed.

There was Chief Tyson Morrow. He'd all but ordered her out of town. But would the chief of police really stoop to vandalism to get rid of her? His hostile reception left little doubt about his feelings toward her.

The sound of tires on gravel pulled her from her thoughts. A patrol car rolled to a stop, and a young officer got out, approaching the house with a notepad in hand.

His eyes tacked from her to the front door and back. "Ma'am? You called about an act of vandalism?"

She gestured to the door and began explaining how she'd come outside and found the message. There wasn't much to her report. The bedrooms were on the second floor of the house at the back to get the view of the lake. Though she'd lain awake most of the night, she hadn't seen or heard anything that might be helpful.

As the officer was completing his report, another vehicle approached, moving quickly up the driveway. Her shoulders tensed as she recognized the police cruiser, and then the broad-shouldered figure emerging from it.

Tyson Morrow.

He strode toward them, the uniform he'd been wearing the night before replaced by snug, well-worn blue jeans and a faded Jill Scott T-shirt. Though his face was inscrutable and his jaw set in a tight, angry line, he was somehow more handsome in the morning light than he'd been the night before. A swell of attraction took root in her chest along with a coil of anger.

"Why are you here?" she demanded before he could speak.

The muscle in his jaw jumped. "I'm the chief of police. I heard we got a call about vandalism at this address."

The patrol officer shifted uncomfortably between them, his gaze darting nervously from his chief to her and back again.

"That still doesn't explain why you're here," she said, suspicion lacing her words.

"I came to check that you were okay." He turned away from her. "Why don't you take a look around the outside of the property," he said to the patrol officer, "then you can head back to the station and type up your report. Have it on my desk before the end of your shift."

"Yes, Chief," the officer replied, eager to escape the tension crackling between them.

Morrow turned back to her, his stance rigid, once the patrolman disappeared. "Is there something you want to say to me?" he barked.

Heat flooded her face, but she didn't back down. "Yesterday, you made it very clear you didn't want me in town. This morning, I wake up to find 'Go home' scrawled on my front door." She gestured toward the vandalized doors, her hand trembling with indignation. "What am I supposed to think?"

The vein in his jaw jumped, a pulse of annoyance beneath his skin. "I'm sure I don't want to tell you what to think," he gritted out, "but I can tell you that I didn't have anything to do with this and, as chief, I will do everything in my power to find out who did."

They stared at each other, the air between them charged

with the implied accusation. Despite her anger, she couldn't help noticing his eyes, gray with little flecks of brown that caught the morning light, eyes that might have been beautiful if they weren't darkened with anger. An inappropriate laugh bubbled in her throat, her body's confused response to the tension. She swallowed it back, knowing her tendency to laugh in awkward moments would only make things worse.

The silence was broken when the patrol officer reappeared around the corner of the house. "Doesn't look like anything else has been disturbed, Chief. I'll head back now." He kept his gaze down as he hurried to his cruiser.

She turned away from Chief Morrow. "I need to go too. I was supposed to meet Stephanie at Amelia's half an hour ago. And I guess now I have to find someone to repaint this door." The thought of her missed breakfast appointment sent a new wave of frustration through her.

"You're going to Amelia's?" he said, unhappy at the news.

She paused at the front door, her hand on the doorknob, looking back over her shoulder. "Yes, Stephanie invited me to breakfast."

He started up the steps. "I don't think—"

She raised her hand, cutting him off. He stopped, surprise momentarily replacing anger on his face. "I don't care what you think, Chief. I'm going to talk to my aunt and cousin, and there's not a thing you can do to stop me."

She turned and walked into the house, closing the door behind her without sparing him another glance, though she couldn't help but feel the weight of his gaze through the wooden panels.

OLIVIA'S MIND WAS still swirling with the image of the message spray-painted on her front doors when she arrived at Amelia's Café. The harsh command to GO HOME had shaken her more than she wanted to admit, but she'd never been a quitter and if there was any chance that her Aunt Amelia could tell her more about her parents, she was going to take it.

Her thoughts went back to the interaction with Tyson Morrow. She wasn't sure why the man got under her skin the way he did, but she couldn't help but feel a twinge of guilt for implying he might have been behind the threatening message. Despite the tension that seemed to arise whenever they were within twenty feet of each other, she'd noticed how thoroughly he had assessed the scene, and his expression of genuine concern for her safety. Whatever his faults, he did appear to be a good cop.

The café's bell jingled as she pushed open the door. The familiar sounds and smells of the café enveloped her as she stepped inside—the hiss of the espresso machine, the murmur of conversation, the rich aroma of coffee beans and fresh pastries. The morning rush was in full swing. She spotted Amelia behind the counter with two other workers bustling around her.

Stephanie weaved between tables, someone's coffee order in hand. She wore a bright yellow apron over her jeans and T-shirt, and her face lit up with genuine pleasure when her gaze landed on Olivia. Stephanie approached and wrapped her in an enthusiastic one-armed hug, careful not to spill the coffee she carried.

"Olivia!" Stephanie exclaimed. "I'm so glad you made it!"

Olivia stiffened, caught off guard by the familiarity. Her adoptive mother had been kind and generous, a caring mother, but physical affection had been rare. Still, there was something about Stephanie that exuded genuine warmth, and she relaxed in her cousin's grip. She stiffly patted Stephanie's back in return.

"Hello, Stephanie. It's good to see you too," she said, her tone more reserved than her cousin's but no less sincere.

"Come on, sit down," Stephanie said, waving toward an empty table by the window. "I'll be right back with lattes for both of us."

Stephanie turned and marched back to the counter before she could mention that she wasn't particularly fond of lattes. She made her way to the indicated table and settled into the chair facing the room.

Stephanie returned to the counter and leaned in to say something to Amelia. The older woman glanced in Olivia's direction, her expression not exactly hostile but not welcoming either.

Olivia mentally prepared herself for another confrontation with her aunt. She understood Amelia's reluctance to discuss the past, but Olivia needed to know the truth about her origins and that outweighed Amelia's discomfort.

The crowd was beginning to thin, leaving a couple lingering over coffee and a few individuals working on laptops. The atmosphere was cozy, the kind of place where Amelia and Stephanie probably knew the regulars' orders by heart. The café was a community gathering place.

Several minutes passed before Stephanie returned, carefully balancing two steaming mugs topped with artful swirls of foam. Olivia accepted the latte with a grateful nod, inhaling the rich aroma. The café door opened again, drawing her attention.

A distinguished-looking man of about sixty stepped inside. He scanned the café with striking blue eyes, his salt-and-pepper hair styled with immaculate precision. His slacks featured a crisp pleat that suggested they were professionally pressed, and even his polo shirt looked like it had been ironed. Unlike most of the casual attire she had seen around Galesburg, this man carried himself with a polished demeanor that reminded her more of the professionals she worked with in DC.

The man's gaze fell on Amelia and his face transformed into a smile so tender and genuine that she could read the emotion behind it without difficulty. The unmistakable look of a man in love. Amelia's face had also softened, the stern lines around her mouth relaxing as she returned the man's smile. She seemed to shed years before Olivia's eyes, momentarily looking like a much younger version of herself.

Beside her, Stephanie tittered. "That happens every time they look at each other," she said with fond exasperation. "I've told Mom, I don't know how many times, to just go ahead and marry that man."

"Who is he?" Olivia asked, fascinated by this glimpse into Amelia's life.

"Tom Fitzgerald. Mom's boyfriend," Stephanie replied, then added quickly, "but she'd have my head if she heard me call him that. She prefers 'friend.'" She rolled her eyes affectionately. "As if anyone with eyes couldn't see they're crazy about each other."

She smiled, thinking of her mother who would have reacted the same way to such a label. Though as far as she knew, her mother had never dated after adopting her. The realization brought a pang of sadness as she realized that her mother had sacrificed that part of her life to focus on raising her.

They watched as Tom crossed the café with purposeful strides, stopping at the counter to say something that made Amelia's smile grow even wider.

Stephanie turned back to Olivia. "Is there someone in your life?" she asked. "Someone that makes you smile like Mom is smiling?"

The question caught her off guard. "No. I don't date much," she said. "Running my business takes up most of my time."

Stephanie took a thoughtful sip of her latte. "I didn't think I had time for love either, not with helping Mom with the café," she said. "But in my experience, love doesn't care whether you have time for it or not."

That hadn't been her experience at all. Love seemed to have little use for her. She dated here and there, but she never seemed to click with anyone. That thought shot a pang of longing and loneliness through her that she pushed away.

Amelia and Tom approached their table, Tom carrying a plate of muffins and Amelia carrying two more coffees. The older couple settled into the chairs across from the younger women, creating a divide across the table.

"I asked Tom to come by for this discussion," Amelia said without preamble. "I wanted someone who would be on my side."

Her shoulders tensed at the words. She hadn't even asked her questions yet, and already Amelia was on the defensive.

Stephanie sighed dramatically. "There are no sides here, Mom," she said. "Olivia just wants to know the truth about her birth. For that matter, so do I. If we are family, we deserve to know it."

Amelia shook her head sadly, her fingers fidgeting with the edge of her napkin. Tom reached over and covered her hand with his own.

"Amelia, honey," he said softly, his voice carrying a gentle encouragement.

Amelia looked at their joined hands for a long moment before exhaling a resigned sigh. "Annalise had a child."

She remained quiet, afraid that any interruption might cause Amelia to stop sharing.

Her aunt raised her eyes to meet Olivia's directly. "I was twenty-three then and she was nineteen and so headstrong." A smile turned up her lips as if she were reliving memories. "She thought she was in love. But he was married."

Olivia let out a breath. Some of the weight that had momentarily lifted returned, settling uncomfortably in her chest. She was the product of an affair between her mother and a married man. The revelation stung.

“I told Annalise she should move on,” Amelia continued. “That he was never going to leave his wife. They never do, but she was blinded by love.” Her voice grew softer. “Around the time she started to see the truth, she found out she was pregnant.”

“That’s why she decided to give me up for adoption?” Olivia asked, unable to keep the note of hurt from her voice. “Because my father didn’t want me?”

Amelia’s expression softened, sympathy replacing her earlier wariness. “You have to understand, Annalise was just a kid herself. Your father, he was older, married and, like I said, never going to leave his wife.” She paused, choosing her next words carefully. “It wasn’t easy for Annalise, but she thought your best chance at a good life would be if she put you up for adoption.”

On some level, she understood what Amelia was saying. But she couldn’t help feeling the sting of rejection. Neither of her birth parents had wanted her enough to keep her. The rational part of her mind argued that her adoptive mother had given her a good life, had loved her unconditionally. She’d never wanted for anything, materially or emotionally. Yet she couldn’t help wondering what life would have been like if her biological parents had kept her.

“Who is my birth father?” Olivia asked, her voice steady despite the turmoil churning inside her.

Amelia shook her head. “I don’t know.”

Stephanie shot her mother a skeptical look, which Amelia immediately caught.

“Don’t look at me like that,” Amelia snapped at her daughter. “I don’t know. Annalise never told me, no matter how hard

I pressed. Whoever he was, he had a hold on her like none of her other boyfriends ever had."

Amelia paused for a moment, collecting herself before continuing. "After Annalise found out she was pregnant, she decided to go away to have the baby. I suspected the father helped her set it up because he didn't want anyone to know she was pregnant and start asking questions. She told everyone she'd won a scholarship to study fashion in New York."

A genuine smile spread across Amelia's face. "Annalise loved clothes. She spent every spare dime she had on fashion magazines, and she had all these drawing books full of her designs." Amelia's gaze fell on Olivia. "Stephanie tells me you're a graphic designer."

"Yes," Olivia confirmed. Her website wasn't hard to find.

Amelia's smile widened. "I'd like to think that's Annalise's influence. She'd be tickled pink to know you have artistic abilities. She was so creative."

She watched as Amelia's smile dimmed. The shared moment of connection made her feel both closer to and further from the mother she'd never known.

"Maybe," Olivia said thoughtfully. "My adoptive mother was an accountant, so not very creative."

Amelia nodded and continued her story. "After Annalise had the baby, she came back to Galesburg. She told everyone that she didn't like the city or the fashion industry as much as she'd thought. I tried to convince her not to come back. To stay in New York and actually go to school. Become the fashion designer she always dreamed of being." She shook her head. "But she wouldn't. She said I was here and Mom and Dad were here in Galesburg. But I knew she hadn't gotten your father out of her system. I think she wanted to, but she just didn't know how."

Olivia tried to put herself in her birth mother's shoes. A

young woman returning to a town where her married lover lived after giving up their child. That couldn't have been easy. She glanced at Amelia and Tom, still holding hands across the table, their connection palpable. Maybe it was a kind of love she had simply never experienced.

"When Annalise got back, she tried to keep her distance, I think, at first," Amelia continued. "She dated a couple other guys, and I thought she'd moved on, but eventually I realized that she was seeing him again."

"The married man?" Olivia asked, wanting to be certain.

Amelia nodded. "She still wouldn't tell me who he was. We argued over it." Her voice caught. "And then, she was gone. Killed in a hit-and-run."

Stephanie reached across the table and took Amelia's other hand, the gesture bridging the divide that had formed earlier. She could see that even after more than thirty years, the loss of her sister still caused Amelia profound pain.

"I'm sorry for your loss," Olivia said, meaning it.

"It's been decades but sometimes it feels like it happened yesterday," Amelia admitted. "Annalise and I were close. I think the only thing we ever disagreed on was…" She stopped abruptly, but Olivia knew what remained unsaid. The only thing they ever disagreed on was her father and her birth.

A complex knot of emotions tightened in her chest—anger at being unwanted, sadness for the mother she'd never know, relief at finally having some answers, and a strange, hollow loss for all the years that could have been different.

"Was anyone ever charged with the hit-and-run?" she asked, trying to piece together the full story.

Stephanie answered this time, her voice gentle. "No. There was never even a suspect. It looks like Aunt Annalise got a flat and stopped on the side of a local road. The police think the driver might not have seen her. The mountain road she was found on didn't have any streetlights."

"This was over three decades ago, before everyone carted around cell phones everywhere," Amelia added. "But our father taught us how to change a tire, and it looked like that was what she was doing when..." She fell silent again, unable to finish the sentence.

Olivia wondered how anyone could hit a person and not know it. Or maybe they had known and simply chosen not to stop. The thought that her birth mother had been left alone on a dark road to die filled Olivia with a cold fury. A mother she would never know, taken from the world before Olivia had any chance to find her.

"That's really all I know," Amelia said, the weariness in her voice reflecting the emotional toll the conversation had taken.

"Thank you," Olivia said sincerely. "I appreciate you sharing with me, and I know it couldn't have been easy."

Amelia nodded and looked directly at her, her expression softening. "You look so much like her."

All her life, she'd looked in mirrors and seen a stranger. She didn't resemble her adoptive mother at all, and she had no idea if she looked like her father. For years she'd studied her own features in mirrors wondering if she'd gotten them from her mother or her father.

Her throat tightened with emotion, and she took a moment to compose herself before speaking again. "I've made a request through the courts to have my adoption files unsealed. I want to find out who my father is."

Amelia's expression immediately shifted to alarm. "I don't know if that is such a good idea."

She cocked her head to the side, surprised by the sudden change. "Why not?"

Amelia's posture grew visibly rigid. "Because whoever

your birth father is, he went through a lot of trouble to keep his identity a secret. He wouldn't want anyone to know his name."

The response sparked a flare of indignation in her. "I don't much care what he wants," she said. "He fathered a child. It's high past time he faced that."

Amelia shook her head emphatically. "This is a small town. It's not like DC, where anything goes. People here still adhere to traditional values. You could be kicking up a storm you don't understand."

Her anger built at Amelia's dismissive attitude. "I understand, but I have a right to know where I come from. Who I come from," she countered, her voice steady but firm. "I can't make my birth father accept me, but I need to know who he is and to look him in the eye and refuse to let him deny my existence any longer."

Amelia stood abruptly, her chair scraping against the floor. "I can't stop you from doing that," she said, her voice tight, "but I don't have to help you."

Without another word, she turned and walked away, with Tom following close behind.

"Mom, wait! Let's talk about this," Stephanie called after her mother.

Amelia didn't respond, disappearing through the door leading into the café's kitchen area.

Stephanie placed her hand over Olivia's. "I'm sorry about that," she said. "Know that I don't agree with Mom. I'll do whatever I can to help, although I don't know how much help I can really be. Most of this is news to me too."

She tried to muster a smile, though she suspected it came out more as a grimace. "Thank you. I appreciate your support."

"Look, I have to get back to work," Stephanie said, glancing at her watch, "but come to dinner at my house tonight."

She glanced back at the kitchen door through which Amelia had disappeared, hesitation evident in her expression.

"Mom won't be there," Stephanie said quickly, reading Olivia's concern. "It will be me and my husband, Geo, and our son, Hanes. I want you to meet them." She paused, then added with deliberate casualness, "And we can take the DNA test if you have the kit with you."

This time, Olivia's smile was genuine, if small. Stephanie's attempt at manipulation wasn't subtle. She wanted the DNA test done, and Stephanie wanted her to come to dinner. It was a fair exchange.

"I do have the kit," Olivia confirmed. "If we take the test tonight, I can send it express to the lab tomorrow morning, and we'll have the results within forty-eight hours of them receiving it. I'm paying for the fastest turnaround they offer."

Stephanie squeezed her hand, her eyes bright with anticipation. "So, in two days or less we will know for sure if we're cousins, but you know what? I don't need a test."

The simple statement spread warmth through her chest and brought a flurry of tears to her eyes. After years of searching and days of cold shoulders in Galesburg, here was someone who welcomed the possibility of their connection.

Stephanie texted her address then excused herself to return to work. Olivia remained at the table, her latte untouched. She turned Stephanie's words over in her mind. In forty-eight hours, she would know for certain if Annalise was her mother. The thought both thrilled and terrified her.

But beneath the anticipation lay a darker current of unease. Someone in this town had spray-painted a threat on her door. Someone wanted her gone before she could discover the truth. And given Amelia's reaction, Olivia couldn't help but wonder if her search might be leading her into deeper, more dangerous waters than she'd anticipated.

What if the man who had abandoned her mother, abandoned them both, was still here in Galesburg? What would he do to keep his secret buried?

She straightened her shoulders, a new resolve hardening within her. She hadn't come this far to be scared away. Whatever secrets Galesburg held about her past, she was determined to uncover them. And she knew just where to start.

Chapter Five

The vandalism report on Olivia's rental house lay open on Tyson's desk, its contents disappointingly sparse. He ran a hand over his face, feeling the stubble that had accumulated since his early morning trek out to the lake. The afternoon sun slanted through the blinds, casting striped shadows across his desk. No evidence found. No witnesses. Nothing but the crude message left behind, and no way to trace who had left it.

"Damn it," he muttered, flipping through the pages again as if additional details might suddenly materialize. The rental property didn't have security cameras, and the neighboring houses were too far away to have captured anything useful. Just dead ends.

He closed the folder and gazed out the window at the town he'd sworn to protect. Main Street stretched below, bathed in golden light of the approaching evening. He didn't like surprises, and the town had more than one in the last twenty-four hours.

He drummed his fingers against the desktop and recalled the conversation he'd had with Amelia after learning about Olivia's arrival in town the day before. Her normally warm, open face had turned to stone the moment he'd mentioned Olivia. It wasn't like Amelia to shut down that way, especially not with him. She'd been his mother's best friend, had practically raised him with his mom alongside Stephanie, and then had folded him right into her family after his mother passed when he was nineteen. He'd always thought of Amelia as a second mother, and he knew she considered him nearly as dear as Stephanie.

"So why the brush off?" he wondered out loud. "What is it about Olivia that has Amelia so rattled?"

His mind drifted to Olivia's face—the high cheekbones, the set of her eyes, the curve of her jaw. The resemblance to Amelia and Stephanie was unmistakable. Her features were fuller, her expressions less open, her attitude more standoffish, but it was undeniable they were related somehow.

A memory stirred from the depths of his childhood—hushed adult conversations and a name spoken with sadness. Amelia had a sister who died when he was just a child. What was her name? Annalise. Annalise who had died young enough that he had no real memory of her. He'd only ever heard her name in passing conversations.

But how young was young? he wondered. Had she been old enough to have had a child before she died?

A stab of guilt pricked him. He'd spent countless hours at Amelia's house growing up, and he knew very little about her life outside of her being a mother and his mother's friend. He couldn't help feeling he should have known more about the sister she lost. But the complex lives of adults weren't the things that children often took notice of.

And as soon as he'd hit his teenage years, all he could think about was escaping Galesburg. The town had felt like a trap then, a place where everyone knew your business and your future was as predictable as the changing of seasons. The navy had been his ticket out. Eight years of service that had shown him parts of the world he'd only seen in magazines. Then college, and after that, he'd joined the Los Angeles police force.

He remembered the congestion of the city, the constant

noise and the anonymity that had once seemed so appealing. Somewhere along the way, that anonymity had changed from feeling like freedom into a distinct feeling of loneliness. The distance from Galesburg had somehow made the town more precious to him. When the chief of police job opened up a year ago, he'd felt a pull he couldn't ignore. The opportunity to serve the community that had raised him, to return to a place where the streets didn't change every year and the people were part of his childhood memories.

He'd been offered this job specifically because he came from outside the department. Galesburg's previous police chief had retired under a cloud of scandal. Nothing that could be proven illegal in court, but following the discovery of a long-ago murder that had been committed and covered up by prominent members in town, the town council had lost faith in the chief's ability to be impartial. The town council had decided they needed someone with no ties to the force, someone who could come in with fresh eyes and restore the integrity that had been lost.

It hadn't hurt that he was a navy veteran who had experience with a major metropolitan police force. Galesburg loved a success story, especially when that success chose to come back home.

Amelia and Stephanie hadn't wasted any time letting him know that they wanted him to settle down with a nice girl, start a family and establish roots in Galesburg that would hold. He knew they were afraid he might wander away again. He wasn't opposed to the idea. He'd always imagined himself with a wife and a couple of kids running around at some point. But that had always been a vision of his future.

"The future has to start sometime," Stephanie had pointed out one evening when he'd expressed the sentiment. She'd fixed him with a look that made him feel transparent and silly simultaneously.

He knew she was right. He couldn't keep putting off starting a family if he really wanted it to happen. But he couldn't imagine raising a family anywhere but Galesburg, and finding the right woman here? That was a challenge. Most women his age were already married. And the ones who weren't he'd known since they were in diapers. It was hard to see romantic potential in someone when you remembered them eating glue in kindergarten or crying over a skinned knee on the playground.

He sighed and reached for the report again. His love life would have to wait. Right now, he had more immediate concerns. Specifically, Olivia Lowell and whoever had decided to leave her that unwelcoming message this morning.

Despite wanting to ensure she wasn't in town to cause problems for Amelia, he knew that unless she broke a law, he didn't have a legal leg to stand on as far as investigating her presence in Galesburg. He tapped his temple, a habit he'd had since childhood when deep in thought. Not having legal cause hadn't prohibited him from doing a little bit of internet sleuthing, though.

His search had yielded surprisingly ordinary results. She was a graphic designer from Washington, DC. Single. No children. No public criminal record. Her social media presence was minimal and entirely professional. A LinkedIn profile highlighting her work with various marketing agencies. An Instagram account featuring mostly design work with the occasional food photo. Nothing that raised any red flags. Nothing that suggested she was anything other than what she appeared to be, a talented professional.

Hardly suspicious. And yet, he couldn't explain his strong reaction to her presence in town. It went beyond his protective instinct for Amelia, though that had certainly been his initial motivation for driving out to the rental property last night. He leaned back in his chair, which creaked in protest. The ceiling fan spun lazily above, stirring the warm afternoon air without actually cooling it.

When he'd been at the lake house the night before, his concern for Amelia had blinded him to some pretty obvious details about Olivia. But in the morning light they'd been impossible to ignore. Olivia standing on the porch with sunlight catching in her chestnut-brown hair, her posture immediately defensive at the sight of his cruiser, her hazel eyes sparking with anger. The visceral attraction to her had caught him completely off guard. And was entirely unprofessional.

And he'd seemed to have had an effect on her as well, though not the kind he was accustomed to. She appeared to loathe him. Her lips pressed into a thin line the moment she'd recognized him.

He couldn't remember ever having that kind of effect on a woman. Frankly, he'd never had a difficult time in the romance department. He was six-two, a few months shy of thirty-seven and he kept himself in admirable shape. Not as good as he'd been during his navy days, maybe, but enough to draw appreciative glances when he jogged through town or swam laps in the community center pool. But her expression had been nothing but hardened stone the entire time he was at the house. And she'd still been drop-dead gorgeous, even with her features twisted into the mother of all frowns.

Olivia might not like him, and she clearly had her own reasons for being in Galesburg that she nor Amelia would share with him, but none of that mattered when it came to protecting her from harassment or threats. He wasn't about to look the other way while someone vandalized her place and tried to intimidate her. That crossed a line.

He studied the photo of the graffiti on Olivia's door. GO HOME. Succinct. Crude black spray paint against the blue door, the letters uneven and hastily formed. Not much to go on. It could have been left by anyone. No, not anyone. Someone who didn't want Olivia hanging around town. He tapped his temple again considering the short list of potential suspects.

The most obvious would be Amelia, given her reaction to Olivia's arrival. But there was no way Amelia would have done this. In all the years he'd known her, he'd never seen her resort to anything remotely underhanded or malicious. She was direct, sometimes brutally so. If Amelia had a problem with you, you knew it. She didn't need spray paint to make her point. Stephanie wouldn't have done it either. She was too kind, too conscious of what others thought of her.

He mentally scrolled through the town's usual troublemakers. The Henderson boys were too young and supervised too closely these days after their last escapade, which had involved a stolen moped. Old man Tucker complained about there being too many tourists in town, but he couldn't see him vandalizing Olivia's rental. There was a group of teenagers who hung out behind the convenience store, but their only crime was loitering. And the biggest problem with all these potential suspects was that they had no motive to target Olivia specifically. As far as he knew, none of them knew her, knew she was in town, or knew where she was staying.

He closed the file, looked up and did a double take. Through the glass walls of his office, he watched Olivia stride through the front doors of the station and stop at the reception desk. Her hair was pulled back in a sleek ponytail, highlighting the lines of her face. Even from this distance, he could see the determined set of her shoulders, the purpose in her stance.

He frowned. Why was she here? Had there been another incident at her rental house?

Usually, the glass front office was too much like working in a fishbowl, but he appreciated being able to keep an eye on his staff, to see the daily operations without having to hover over anyone's shoulder. And he appreciated it now as he watched Revis, the newest addition to the force, speak with Olivia. The young officer nodded, picked up the phone, and Tyson's desk phone buzzed a moment later.

"Yes."

"Chief, there is a Miss Lowell here to see you," Revis said, his voice carrying the careful formality of a new officer still finding his footing. "She doesn't have an appointment though."

"That's alright, Revis. Send her on back."

He replaced the receiver and stood, smoothing the tie in his uniform as he did. He generally kept a tidy office, but the number of files that always seemed to need his review just kept piling up. He couldn't stand to have stacks of them on his desk, so he'd taken to putting them in the visitors' chairs. That kept his desk clear and also discouraged lingering in his office, a practical approach to time management that Stephanie had once told him was "borderline antisocial." He'd rolled his eyes at her and stacked another pile of files in the chair.

He grabbed a stack of files from one of the chairs now and placed it on top of the file cabinet just as a knock sounded on the glass door to the office. Crossing the room in two steps, he pulled the door open.

Olivia stood there, close enough that he could smell the faint scent of honey and ginger. Her gaze was steady, direct and decidedly cool.

"Miss Lowell," he said, aiming for professional detachment despite the odd flutter in his chest. "I'm afraid we haven't found the person who vandalized your rental home yet."

She stepped into his office, her movements careful and contained. She stopped just past the threshold, as if reluctant to commit fully to being in his space. "I'm sure you're doing the best you can," she said, her tone suggesting she might not actually believe the words but knew they were the polite ones to offer, "but that is not why I'm here."

He gestured toward the chair he'd just cleared. "Please have a seat." He noticed the slight hesitation before she moved forward, lowering herself into the visitor's chair with the same deliberate control that seemed to characterize all her movements.

He settled behind his desk, the familiar position grounding him, reminding him of his role. "What can I do for you?" He studied her face. There was something different about her expression. A vulnerability that hadn't been there that morning, partially hidden behind a carefully constructed wall of composure.

She took a deep breath and let it out slowly. The deliberate action made him tense.

"I spoke with Amelia," she began, her fingers twisting together in her lap. "I learned some things about my mother. About the woman I believe to be my birth mother."

His interest sharpened instantly. "Okay," he said, keeping his voice even, encouraging.

"I believe my birth mother was Annalise and that Amelia is my aunt." Her voice grew steadier as she continued, as if saying the words aloud gave her strength. "Amelia confirmed that her sister did give birth to a baby girl when she was nineteen and that she gave that baby up for adoption."

He couldn't hide his surprise. His eyebrows rose, and his mouth opened before he caught himself. His mind raced, connecting dots.

"You didn't know?" Olivia asked, keen eyes catching his reaction.

He shook his head. "No. I knew Amelia had a sister that passed away years ago, but I was still very young when that happened." He leaned forward, resting his forearms on the desk. "And Amelia doesn't talk about the past much."

Olivia nodded, a flicker of something crossing her face. "That tracks with everything I've seen of Amelia so far." She paused, seemingly gathering her thoughts. "Amelia explained that Annalise was seeing a married man. When he found out she was pregnant, he sent Annalise off to New York to have the baby and give it up for adoption."

Tyson absorbed this new information. The pieces fit. Amelia's reaction to Olivia's arrival, the physical resemblance between them, her determination to be in Galesburg despite the less than warm welcome. It all made sense now.

"Did Amelia tell you who the father was?" he asked, already suspecting the answer from the shadow that passed over her face.

Olivia's expression darkened, and she shook her head. "No. Amelia says that Annalise never told her, and despite everything, I believe her."

"I take it you plan on finding out who your birth father is."

It wasn't really a question. He could see the determination in the set of her jaw, the focus in her eyes.

She nodded once, decisively. "Yes, but that is not why I've come to see you." She hesitated for a moment, her fingers now still in her lap, as if she'd moved beyond nervousness into resolution. "Amelia said that Annalise was killed in a hit-and-run. I'd like to see the police file on the case."

He sat up straighter. "A hit-and-run?"

Olivia seemed surprised by his reaction. "Yes. That's what Amelia said." Her eyes narrowed. "You didn't know about that either?"

His mind raced back through fragmented childhood memories. "I'd heard that Annalise was killed in a car accident, but hit-and-run implies something criminal." He chose his words carefully. "That would mean someone was responsible."

"Well, all I know is what Amelia told me," she said, her voice steady despite the emotion he could see building behind her eyes. "And she used the words 'hit-and-run.'"

He nodded slowly. If Annalise had been killed in a hit-and-run, there should be a police file. There would have been an investigation, maybe even suspects. And if the case had never been solved…

"How long ago did Annalise die?" he asked, mentally calculating backward. If Olivia was in her early thirties, and Annalise had been nineteen when she gave birth…

"Thirty-four years ago," she replied, swallowing hard before she continued speaking. "Apparently, it wasn't that long after I was given up for adoption."

Tyson turned to the laptop on his desk and began typing, searching the computerized records for Annalise's name. When the file appeared, he opened it and scanned quickly, confirming that Annalise Farr had indeed been killed in an apparent hit-and-run on Route 360. More troublingly, it was technically a cold case and still open. Someone had gone unpunished for more than thirty years.

He turned back to Olivia, his mind racing. "It does appear that Annalise was killed in a hit-and-run accident." He tapped his temple again. "But letting you review the file, that's unorthodox."

Her spine stiffened visibly, and Tyson could see her bristling for an argument. "The case has gone unsolved for over three decades and you, the chief of police, didn't even know about it. I hardly think letting me see the file could hurt your chances of solving it."

Her words stung, partly because she was right. He should have known about the cold case. As chief, every unsolved crime in Galesburg was his responsibility, even those that predated him.

"Look," Olivia continued, her voice softening, "I've always felt as though a part of me was missing. I've never really known where or who I've come from. My birth mother didn't want me to know, and now I find that my aunt isn't all that forthcoming. This is something I can know about my birth mother, however unpleasant it might be."

"Unpleasant" didn't begin to cover it. Galesburg's department lacked the resources to digitize files as old as this case, but the paper records would be in the basement archives. They would likely include photographs and various other disturbing pieces of evidence. Hit-and-runs were gruesome business.

He studied Olivia across the desk. While he understood her desire to learn about her birth mother, he questioned whether viewing such traumatic material was in her best interest. But when he looked into her eyes and saw the mixture of longing and determination there, he knew he would yield to her request. At least partially.

"Okay," he said after a long pause, "but I'm going to be with you, and I need to review the pages first. I can't promise you I'll let you see the entire file, or any of it for that matter. If there is anything thing in there that I feel showing you might jeopardize a future case against the perpetrator, I will hold it back. Agreed?"

For the first time since they'd met, a genuine smile spread across her face. The transformation was stunning, sending an unexpected jolt through his system that nearly knocked him from his chair.

"Agreed," she said, and that single word seemed to shift the air between them, forging a bridge across the chasm of suspicion and dislike.

He stood, ignoring the warmth spreading through his chest. "The archives are in the basement."

"Then let's go," she replied, rising from her chair. "I'm ready for some answers."

Chapter Six

The door to Tyson's office closed behind them with a soft click, and Olivia followed him through the labyrinth of desks toward the elevator, neither of them speaking. He pressed the down button, and they got on the elevator, standing side by side, watching the numbered display above tick down. She stole a glance at his profile, his crooked nose, the slight furrow between his brows that seemed to be a permanent feature, the set of his square jaw that suggested a man that didn't smile nearly enough. She wondered if he would actually follow through on showing her the file on her birth mother's hit-and-run, or if this would all be for nothing.

Why was she even doing this? She watched her reflection in the brushed steel of the elevator doors. The woman looking back at her seemed looked haggard and exhausted. What did she really expect to find in a file this old? Certainly not answers as to why her mother had given her up at birth. Or why Amelia seemed to want nothing to do with her.

But she knew why. She needed to know her birth mother. In whatever capacity she could. Even if it hurt.

There was little she knew about Annalise Farr. But how she died, and maybe why, was something she could know. Something Amelia couldn't keep her from discovering.

But beyond the desire to know was a deeper reason. The idea that no one had ever been held accountable for Annalise's death didn't sit well with her. Even if Annalise's death had been nothing more than a tragic accident, the person responsible should have answered for that. No one deserved to be forgotten the way it seemed Annalise had been. And if it was truly an accident, why hadn't the person helped?

The elevator jerked to a stop, interrupting her thoughts before they could spiral into darker territory. The doors opened with a ding.

She stepped out behind Tyson and blinked in surprise. She'd expected a space that was dim and dusty, the kind of basement that featured in crime shows, concrete walls and flickering fluorescent lights. Instead, she found herself in a bright, clean hallway with recessed lighting and freshly painted walls. The air was cool but not damp, with none of the mustiness she'd anticipated. The basement was remarkably quiet compared to the bullpen, where phones rang constantly and officers had moved about, their voices creating a constant background hum. Down here, their footsteps seemed to be the only sound.

She followed Tyson through the halls, noting the occasional door as they passed. Storage. Property. Evidence Processing. Her heartbeat quickened as they turned a corner and approached a door marked Archives.

Beside the door was black square. Tyson reached into his shirt pocket and removed what looked like a white credit card, swiping it. Another buzz and the door clicked and unlocked.

"Welcome to where old cases go to rest," Tyson said, pushing the door open and holding it for her.

Olivia stepped inside, taking in the room with its metal shelves lining the walls. Each shelf held cardboard boxes of varying sizes, all of them labeled with red marker in neat handwriting. She estimated there were about thirty boxes total, each one representing someone's tragedy. Someone's loss. Someone's crime.

The thought made her sad.

"Are these all unsolved cases?" she asked.

Tyson closed the door behind them. "No. Until today I didn't know there were any unsolved cases in Galesburg." He frowned, and she could tell he wasn't happy about that realization. He did seem to care about his job and she could respect that, even if the man rubbed her the wrong way.

"We are required to keep the evidence from the cases we investigate until all appeals are exhausted," he continued. "We don't have a lot of crime in Galesburg, but it does add up over time."

She ran her eyes over the boxes, each one labeled with a case number, year and name. Some dated back to the 1980s, others as recent as the past few years. Somewhere among them was a box containing the name of her birth mother.

She wrapped her arms around herself, cold despite the perfectly regulated climate. She hadn't expected to feel this way. As if she were standing on the edge of a precipice, about to take a step that couldn't be taken back.

But it was too late for second thoughts. Tyson was down the aisle, eyes scanning the labels on the boxes, and she followed him. The fluorescent lights hummed overhead, casting everything in a flat, unforgiving brightness that reminded her of hospital corridors. Their footsteps echoed against the concrete floor, marking their progress through the archives of Galesburg's darker moments. The boxes were arranged in chronological order, the years marching backward as they moved deeper into the room. It didn't take long to find the box they were looking for.

"Here it is," Tyson said, stopping near the end of the aisle.

Her breath caught as Tyson pulled an unremarkable white cardboard box off the shelf with "Farr, Annalise, September 20, 1995" written on the side in red marker.

"Let's see what we have," Tyson said, turning and walking toward a metal desk positioned against the far wall.

He set the box down, but she stood rooted to the spot for a moment, unsure if she was ready for what came next.

"Have a seat," Tyson instructed, gesturing to the single chair at the desk. "I'll grab another chair for myself."

She moved to the desk and lowered herself into the chair. He was already stretching rules to accommodate her, so she suppressed the urge to tear it open and waited for him to come back.

She could hear him moving something then the scrape of metal against concrete before he reappeared carrying a metal folding chair. He set it up beside, her heat jumping a bit as he sat and reached for the box.

Inside lay a slender manila file and a clear plastic evidence bag containing what appeared to be a dirty yellow sweater. Nothing else.

Tyson's mouth pulled downward as he surveyed the contents.

"What?" she asked.

He shook his head. "I just expected more."

The disappointment in his voice mirrored her own feelings. The box's contents seemed inadequate to have been a full investigation of Annalise's death.

Tyson opened the file and she instinctively scooted her chair closer to his, eager to see what few documents might illuminate her mother's last hours. To her frustration, he immediately shifted away, angling the papers so she couldn't easily read it.

"I want to read over it first," he said, not looking at her. "I told you, I may not be able to show you everything."

A flare of irritation rose in her chest. She'd come this far, only to be kept at arm's length from the very information she sought. His eyes moved across the pages, which she could see consisted of only about two sheets of paper.

His frown deepened into a scowl, the furrow between his brows growing more pronounced. “The police report is sparse.”

“Sparse?” she repeated, leaning forward again despite his earlier withdrawal.

“Yeah.” Tyson’s jaw tightened. “I know they didn’t have access to the same kinds of technologies that we do now, but I would have expected to find forensic drawings of the scene and at least some attempt to seek out witnesses. Maybe someone drove by on the road and saw something, but there’s nothing to indicate that in the report.”

“But that wasn’t done?” she asked, though she knew the answer from his expression.

Tyson tossed the report on the table face down. “No. It wasn’t,” he said, disgust evident in every word.

He picked up the other document in the file and held it at an angle that prevented her from seeing its contents. His protective posture sent a fresh wave of irritation through her.

“By law, I’m entitled to see the autopsy report,” she said, grateful for the hasty research she’d done on her phone before coming to see him. “At least let me see that.”

He gave her a sharp look, his eyes narrowing. “A direct relative has the right to view the autopsy report. It hasn’t been established that you are Annalise’s biological daughter.”

The words stung. Still, after coming this far, she refused to be shut out on a legal technicality. She glared at him.

Tyson held her gaze for a long moment, some internal calculation happening behind his eyes. Then his expression softened almost imperceptibly. “Fine. We can look at it together.”

He pushed the autopsy report over so they could both read

it. She leaned in, and he did the same, their shoulders nearly touching. She caught his scent, leather and whiskey.

The thought fled as she focused on the report before her. The medical terminology was unfamiliar, but at the bottom of the page was the printed figure of a woman. It was marked with various notations and indicators that she couldn't fully interpret, but she'd seen enough crime shows on television to pick up on what they likely meant. Annalise's body had suffered extensive bruising. Something that was easy to understand was the cause of death, typed on the appropriate line. Blunt force trauma to the head. And beside it, the manner of death. Homicide.

She touched the word *homicide*, and her breath came out in a little hiccup. The black ink seemed to darken beneath her fingertip, as if responding to her touch. A strange buzzing began behind her ears, her vision narrowing to that single word on the page.

"That just indicates that the death was caused by someone else," Tyson said, as if he could read on her face where her thoughts were taking her. "It doesn't necessarily mean that anyone can be criminally prosecuted, although…"

His voice trailed off, and her attention shifted from the report to his face. His brows were drawn together, creating deep furrows in his forehead as he studied the diagram.

"Although, what?"

His gaze remained fixed on the autopsy report, as if he were reluctant to voice what he was thinking. The silence stretched between them.

He looked at her. "This autopsy report is concerning," he said, each word measured and deliberate.

Her fingers curled around the edge of the desk, the metal cool against her skin. "Concerning how?" she pressed, needing him to be explicit, to confirm or deny the terrible suspicion that was taking shape in her mind.

He hesitated again, and she watched the internal struggle play out across his features. He seemed to make a decision. He scooted a fraction of an inch closer to her, bringing the pages with him.

"You see here," he said, pointing to the drawn figure on the top of the second page. "The coroner listed the cause of death as blunt force trauma to the head."

"Yes, well, isn't that common in cases of hit-and-run?" she asked. She didn't know much about such injuries, but it seemed logical that being struck by a vehicle would cause head trauma.

"It's not unusual," he acknowledged, "but see here." She followed his finger as he dragged it to the bottom of the page, to the markings on the diagram. "It says that there were multiple head injuries. At least three. Including two to the back of her head."

She stared at where he was pointing, trying to make sense of the medical shorthand. The room seemed to grow colder as the implication of his words began to take shape in her mind. The pieces assembled themselves with terrible clarity.

Her heart raced, each pulse thundering in her ears.

"In a typical vehicle strike," he continued, "we'd expect to see a single point of impact, consistent with the height of the vehicle's bumper or hood. Secondary injuries might occur when the victim falls to the ground, but they follow a pattern dependent upon if the victim rolled, hit something, or stayed where they landed."

She watched his face as he spoke with the detached precision of a professional, but his tone suggested this was more than academic to him.

"This pattern of injuries," he said, tapping the diagram again, "is inconsistent with being struck by a vehicle. The angle of the impacts, particularly those to the back of the head…they suggest something else entirely."

The buzzing in her ears intensified, but she was unable to look away from the clinical drawing that represented her mother's broken body.

"What are you saying?" she said softly.

Somewhere in the basement, a door slammed. The world continued to turn while she held her breath, waiting for an answer that would irrevocably change everything.

Tyson looked up from the report, his eyes meeting hers directly. There was compassion there, but also an honesty that told her he wouldn't soften the truth.

"I think there's a good chance that Annalise's death wasn't caused by a hit-and-run, but someone sure wanted it to look that way."

Her body went rigid, her lungs seizing, unable to take in air for several long moments. Not an accident. Not a random tragedy. But deliberate. Someone had killed her mother and disguised it as a traffic accident. And for more than thirty years, no one had questioned it. No one had looked closely enough at these same documents to see what Tyson had seen in minutes.

Olivia looked down at her hands, which trembled in her lap. "If what you're saying is true, then someone got away with murder. Someone in this town."

The words hung in the air between them. Tyson didn't contradict her. His silence was confirmation that he'd been thinking the same thing.

"I need to know what happened," she said, the tremor in her hands spreading to her voice. "I need to know who did this to her."

Tyson nodded. "Me too. As of right now, Annalise Farr's cold case has been reopened."

Chapter Seven

Olivia clutched the expensive bottle of cabernet in her hands as she stared at Stephanie's front door. The porch light cast a warm glow on the welcome mat, but her feet remained rooted to the concrete step. She'd worked with difficult vendors and unreasonable clients without breaking a sweat, yet now she was paralyzed by the prospect of small talk.

Get it together, girl.

Socializing had never been her strong suit. Back in Washington, she'd developed a comfortable routine that minimized forced interactions—work, home, occasional drinks with friends who knew her well enough that conversation flowed easily.

Stephanie was the only person here who didn't look at her like she was an intruder, and Stephanie had invited her to dinner. *You can do this.*

She straightened her spine, squared her shoulders and pressed the doorbell. The melodic chime had barely finished its tune when the door swung open, revealing Stephanie's beaming face.

"Olivia! You made it!" Stephanie pulled her into an exuberant hug.

The unexpected warmth of the embrace startled a laugh from Olivia. Stephanie's enthusiasm was like a gust of fresh air, blowing away her anxiety. "Of course I made it. Thank you for inviting me."

"Get in here." Stephanie tugged her inside, closing the door with her foot in one practiced motion. "Everyone's here. Almost everyone."

She let herself be guided through the home's entryway, her boots clicking against the hardwood floors. Family photos lined the walls. Stephanie with a man Olivia presumed was Geo and a boy at holiday gatherings. It was a home filled with memories and connections.

Stephanie led her to the threshold of a living room where three sets of eyes immediately turned to assess her. A flush crept up Olivia's neck, along with renewed anxiety, as she stood on display.

"Everyone, this is Olivia. Olivia's visiting us from Washington, DC," Stephanie announced, her hand still firmly gripping her cousin's elbow. "Olivia, this is my husband, Geo, his father, Marcus, and our little monster Hanes, who is four going on forty."

Geo rose from his armchair, a tall man with a runner's build and kind brown eyes that crinkled at the corners when he smiled. "Welcome to our home, Olivia."

Marcus, silver-haired and robust with the same brown eyes as his son, lifted his glass in greeting. "It's a pleasure to meet you, young lady."

The little boy remained focused on a set of building blocks on the carpet, completely ignoring the introduction. His tongue darted in and out of his mouth as he meticulously stacked one block atop another.

"It's nice to meet you all." Olivia lifted the wine bottle like an offering. "Thank you for having me over. I brought this to say thanks."

Geo stepped forward to take the bottle, his eyebrows rising

as he examined the label. “Oh, it’s the good stuff! I’ll get more glasses.” His easy teasing broke the tension in her shoulders.

Geo disappeared toward what Olivia assumed was the kitchen as the doorbell’s chime cut through the momentary lull in conversation.

“That’ll be our last guest.” Stephanie squeezed Olivia’s arm before turning back toward the door. “Make yourself comfortable.”

Marcus patted the couch cushion beside him. “So, Olivia from Washington, DC, what do you do?”

She perched on the couch. “I’m a graphic designer, mainly working with corporate clients.”

“Is that so?” Marcus’s eyes lit up with interest. “Creating logos and such? I always wished I had more of a creative streak, but there’s not a creative bone in my body.” He chuckled, a deep rumbling sound that emanated from his barrel chest. “So, I became a judge instead. Get to wear a fancy robe and tell people what to do all day. Not a bad consolation prize.”

She found herself relaxing even more at his self-deprecating humor, which she suspected was the judge’s goal. Movement on the other side of the room caught her attention. Her smile froze as her gaze landed on Tyson standing in the doorway. He nodded almost imperceptibly in greeting, his face as unreadable as ever.

The surprise must have shown on her face because Stephanie shot her a somewhat apologetic glance as she came to sit next to her. “I needed a sixth to make the numbers even,” she explained in a hurried whisper.

Olivia had left the police department not long after Tyson had declared he’d be reopening her mother’s hit-and-run case, relieved, and with a renewed sense of purpose. But she hadn’t expected to see him again so soon. Something about his presence here, in Stephanie's cozy home and him out of uniform, threw her off-kilter.

Marcus leaned into their conversation, oblivious to the tension. "Hanes is my date for the night." He burst into laughter at his own joke, the sound filling the awkward silence.

"Everybody mingle," Stephanie announced, her voice overly bright. "Dinner will be ready soon. I'm just going to go check on it." She slipped away toward the kitchen, leaving Olivia stranded in a room with Marcus and Tyson, who still hovered uncomfortably near the entryway.

Geo returned carrying the opened wine bottle and a cluster of stemmed glasses pinched between his fingers. "Who wants a taste? Olivia brought us something special." He poured the ruby liquid into wineglasses. She accepted a glass from Geo, grateful she had in fact sprung for the good stuff.

Stephanie called them to dinner a moment later. They migrated to the dining room, where a rectangular oak table gleamed under warm pendant lights. Mismatched cloth napkins in jewel tones brightened each place setting, and the centerpiece, a simple arrangement of summer flowers in a blue ceramic pitcher, added casual elegance to the scene. The room smelled like roasted chicken and herbs. She settled into her assigned seat, noting with a mix of relief and tension that Tyson sat across and one seat over, not directly in her line of sight. Stephanie carried in steaming dishes while Geo carved the chicken at the head of the table. The domestic choreography unfolded with such natural ease that she suspected that friends gathered around this table often, sharing food and conversation. She accepted a bowl of roasted vegetables, momentarily overwhelmed by an unexpected pang of longing for the sense of belonging that Stephanie and Geo seemed to have.

Over dinner, Marcus guided the conversation from topic to topic with the same deftness he likely employed in his courtroom, and Marcus had a gift for making everyone feel included without putting them on the spot. The father-son tag team hosting approach created a comfortable atmosphere. She found herself laughing at Marcus's colorful stories about small-town judicial life and contributing her own anecdotes about demanding design clients without the self-consciousness that typically shadowed her social interactions. The wine continued to flow generously with dinner, a different bottle now, a lighter wine that Geo explained came from a nearby vineyard.

Tyson had unbuttoned his collar and looked relaxed, although his contributions to the conversation were still sparse. A man of few words. She also noted the subtle softening around his eyes when Hanes launched into a dissertation about the ongoing saga of who got to be line leader at his preschool and the tragedy of spilled juice at snack time. And the slight upward tilt at the corners of his mouth when Marcus delivered a particularly outlandish punchline. There was more than just a coldhearted chief of police in there, she thought. Maybe one day he'd show her this other side.

Woah, where did that come from? She didn't need Tyson Morrow showing her any side of himself. She was in Galesburg to discover who her birth father was and, maybe, forge the beginnings of a relationship with her aunt and cousin. Chief Tyson Morrow didn't enter into that equation at all.

After they'd all finished dessert, slices of homemade apple pie topped with vanilla ice cream that melted into sweet puddles, Geo rose, looking at Stephanie pointedly. "You cooked. Hanes and I will clean up." He leaned in, pressing a kiss to Stephanie's cheek, his eyes conveying affection more significant than simple husbandly courtesy.

Stephanie hesitated, a silent exchange passing between them that Olivia couldn't quite decipher but recognized as the wordless communication of a long-married couple.

"Dad can help," Geo added, glancing toward his father.

Marcus pushed his chair back with a theatrical scrape. "I'll supervise," he announced, bringing his half-full wineglass with him as he stood. His eyes twinkled with mischief, the laugh lines around them deepening. "And, Tyson, you can police us all and make sure we're doing our jobs right." He gestured expansively with his free hand. "Everyone can play to their strengths."

Marcus's deep laugh rumbled through the dining room as Geo lifted Hanes from his booster seat. The boy's small head nodded against his father's shoulder, eyelids heavy despite his earlier insistence that he wasn't tired. The three of them moved toward the kitchen doorway, leaving Tyson still seated. He remained motionless, his fingers tracing the condensation on his water glass. He pushed back his chair and stood, his eyes met Olivia's briefly before he turned and followed the path the others had taken. The swinging door to the kitchen fluttered shut behind him, leaving Olivia and Stephanie alone in the dining room.

Stephanie turned to Olivia, her voice dropping to a near whisper despite the buffer of distance and running water from the kitchen. "I thought now would be a good time to do the DNA test. Geo has orders to keep Hanes busy."

So that was the message that passed between the couple. "Yeah, now is great." Olivia pushed her chair back and stood, smoothing her slacks with her palms. "I brought the test kits with me. Thank you for doing this."

She and Stephanie moved from the dining room back through to the living room where Olivia had left her purse on a side table near the entry. She retrieved her bag, extracting a white box with clinical blue lettering. The packaging was nondescript. Olivia handled it carefully.

"It's really simple," she explained as she opened the box.

Inside were two sealed packages containing cotton swabs, each with a plastic tube attached. "We just have to swab the inside of our cheeks and then seal the swabs in these tubes."

Stephanie nodded, watching intently as Olivia demonstrated by tearing open one of the packages. The plastic crinkled loudly in the quiet room.

Olivia watched Stephanie mirror her, swiping the cotton along her inner cheek. Stephanie finished and sealed her sample, then handed it back to Olivia with a solemnity that acknowledged the gravity of what they were doing. Olivia placed both tubes back into the protective pouch provided in the kit.

"I'll send these off first thing in the morning," Olivia said, sealing the pouch and returning it to her purse.

"That's great. Although, I already know the answer." Stephanie smiled and squeezed Olivia's hand. "There's something I want to give to you."

Stephanie turned and moved toward the hallway that branched off from the living room. The corridor walls were lined with more family photos, beach vacations, wedding photos and photos of Hanes that chronicled the evolution of this family through the years. At the end of the hall, Stephanie pushed open a door that revealed a study. Unlike the rest of the house with its deliberate coziness, this room had the slightly chaotic energy of a space used for multiple purposes. Toys littered the floor in one corner. A book lay open and face down on a reclining chair in another corner and a rolltop desk occupied one wall, a desk lamp casting a pool of amber light over the surface, which was cluttered with paper.

A cardboard box sat in the center of the desk. Unlike the evidence box from earlier in the day, this one had no lid. A slim book with a faded spine poked up over the side along with a plush and colorful Care Bear, what looked like a drawing pad, and a fabric pencil case.

Stephanie crossed to the desk and placed one hand on the box, her fingers curling protectively around its worn corner. “I remembered that I accidentally took this box with me when I moved out of Mom’s house.” Her voice carried a hint of apology, as if she’d been keeping something valuable from Olivia intentionally. “It’s some of Aunt Annalise’s things that Mom kept. I thought you might like to have it.”

Annalise’s things. Tangible pieces of a life cut short, objects that had been touched and cherished by the mother she’d never known. Olivia approached the desk.

The purple Care Bear stared up at her from inside the box, a heart emblazoned on its round belly. The teddy bear’s fur was matted in places from years of handling, one ear bent as if it had been a favorite spot to hold. She lifted it from the box as carefully as if it were made of glass rather than polyester and stuffing. The toy had been important enough to Annalise that she’d kept it into adulthood, a childhood comfort carried forward into her nineteenth year. Olivia tried to reconcile this innocent object with the sparse facts she knew about her mother—nineteen, pregnant, murdered. The bear had a story. Had it been a gift? A purchase made with saved allowance? A comfort object during childhood illnesses or the turbulence of adolescence? These were questions that might never have answers. Olivia glanced at Stephanie, who watched her with soft eyes, but even she might not know the bear’s significance. And Amelia had barely been willing to acknowledge Olivia’s existence, let alone share childhood memories.

“I don’t know much about Aunt Annalise,” Stephanie said, as if reading Olivia’s thoughts. “Mom said the family donated most of Annalise’s things after...” She trailed off, the unspoken tragedy hanging in the air between them. “I found this box years later when I was looking for some old school records. Mom must have missed it when she was clearing Aunt Annalise's things away."

Olivia nodded. Grief made people do strange things. Some preserved rooms like shrines, others erased every trace of the person they'd lost. Amelia and her parents had apparently chosen the latter path, but somehow this box had escaped the purge. These few objects were bridges to a past that Annalise hadn't wanted Olivia to be a part of.

"Thank you," Olivia said, the words inadequate for the gift Stephanie had given her. Not just the objects themselves but the connection to Annalise. "It means more than I can say."

The sound of a glass shattering followed by Hanes's startled cry and Marcus's booming reassurance that accidents happen pulled Stephanie's attention from Olivia.

"I'd better go see about them before they destroy my kitchen." Stephanie leaned in and gave Olivia a quick hug before leaving the room.

She barely had time to register Stephanie's departure before another presence filled the doorway. Tyson stood there, his broad shoulders nearly touching both sides of the frame, his expression not hiding his interest in what she was doing.

A smirk formed on Olivia's lips. "Eavesdropping, Chief? I'd have expected better of you."

Chapter Eight

Tyson gave a smile, leaning against the doorframe. "I'm not above eavesdropping when it serves my purposes, but no. I was coming to get Stephanie at Geo's request." The wood was solid against his shoulder, grounding him as his eyes drifted to the cardboard box on the desk. "What is that?"

"Stephanie had some things of Annalise's that she thought I might like to have." Olivia's voice had a careful neutrality to it, but her fingers tightened almost imperceptibly around the box's edge.

"That was nice of her."

Olivia's attention shifted to the bookshelf beside her, where a framed photograph sat among leather-bound books and decorative objects. He recognized it as a picture of Stephanie, Geo and Hanes, all three beaming at the camera from a backdrop of summer sky. "She is nice," Olivia said with a smile that transformed her face, brightened her eyes. But almost as quickly as it appeared, the smile faltered.

"What are you thinking?" he asked, surprised by his own question. It wasn't his place to probe, and yet he couldn't help himself.

Olivia fidgeted with the box. "Stephanie is so nice. And so are Geo and Marcus. And even Hanes has to be the cutest four-year-old on the planet. And I'm…" Her voice trailed off, leaving the thought incomplete.

You're perfect, he thought, the words forming in his mind with such clarity that for a moment he feared he'd spoken them aloud. *Where did that come from? You don't even know the woman.*

He blinked, unsettled by his own reaction. This wasn't like him, this immediate, visceral response to someone he barely knew, someone who was connected to a case, no less.

"You're what?" he prompted.

Olivia sighed heavily, the sound seeming to come from somewhere deep inside her. "I don't even know who I am." The admission hung in the air between them.

"Yes, you do," he shot back, the words emerging before he could weigh them. "You're a talented graphic designer and a successful businesswoman." The facts came easily to him; he'd done his research, of course. That was the job. What wasn't part of the job was the desire to remind her of her own worth.

A smile played at Olivia's lips, not quite reaching her eyes. "Checked up on me, huh."

He returned the smile. "It is my job."

"And you are good at it," she replied.

"I am," he said. Their eyes met and held, and something passed between them, a moment of understanding.

Olivia sighed again, but this time the sound was more tired than weary, as if she were setting down a weight she'd been carrying. "I guess I'm just overwhelmed. It was always just my mother and me. I'm not used to family dinners like this." She gestured vaguely, seeming to indicate not just the house but the entire concept of extended family gathered together.

He moved farther into the room, drawn by her vulnerability. "I can see how it can be overwhelming if you're not used to it." He remembered his first holiday after his mother died, how wrong it had felt to be at Amelia's table, surrounded by her family's easy warmth when his own family had been reduced to fragments.

"Are you from a big family?"

He laughed, the sound surprising him with its genuine mirth. "I guess you could say that. I'm from Galesburg." The reference to the notoriously large, tight-knit community was an old joke, but one that still amused him.

Olivia laughed with him, her shoulders relaxing. The sound of her laughter was unexpectedly pleasant and crinkled the corners of her eyes.

"I have an older sister," he continued, moving to stand closer to her. "She lives in Boston. I see her a few times a year. But Amelia and Stephanie are like family." He was sharing more than he normally would. "Amelia and my mother were best friends. My mother passed from a sudden aneurysm when I was nineteen."

The memories of her still had sharp edges that could cut if he approached it wrong, but time had smoothed some of the sharpness away, leaving a dull ache in its place.

"I'm sorry," Olivia said, the words simple but sincere.

"Thank you," he said with a nod, acknowledging her sympathy without dwelling on it. "My sister is seven years older and was already off in Boston, and I was a little lost. Amelia had always been like a second mother to me, and she took me under her wing. Took care of me. Really helped me through the initial grief."

He rarely spoke about this period of his life, that strange limbo between being someone's child and being truly on his own. The US Navy and then the police academy had given him structure, but Amelia had given him permission to feel, to grieve, to eventually heal.

"I'm glad you had someone," she said, and there was a hint of longing in her voice, that made him wonder about her own support system. Who had been there for her in her darkest moments?

He stepped closer to her, drawn by an impulse he couldn't name. He was suddenly aware of the space between them, close enough that in any other context it might be considered inappropriate, intimate even. But she didn't back away, and he couldn't bring himself to step back. Something pulled him toward her, an intense need to be close that wasn't rational.

"I know you haven't received the reception from Amelia that you hoped to receive," he said, "but give it time. She really is a special person. And I can tell you are as well. I'm sure she'll come around."

A charged moment, passed between them. Her fingers stilled on the box, and the floral faint scent that might have been her shampoo or perfume tickled his nose. He was undeniably attracted to her, and he was fairly sure he saw the same attraction in her eyes reflected back at him.

What would it be like to kiss her? His gaze dropped to her lips for just a fraction of a second before he caught himself.

Movement in the doorway broke the moment. They both turned to find Hanes standing there, watching them with the unselfconscious curiosity that only children possessed.

"Whatcha doing?" the boy asked, his face a picture of innocent inquiry.

Olivia laughed nervously, the sound breathless.

Tyson silently thanked Hanes for stopping him from doing something incredibly stupid. Whatever had been building between them, whatever line he'd been about to cross, remained undisturbed.

He crossed to the door and scooped Hanes up, grateful for the distraction and the return to safer ground. "Hey, you promised me you'd show me your new Lego set. You're not reneging on a promise, are you?" He tickled the boy's sides, making him squirm and giggle.

"No, no. I'm not reneging." Hanes laughed uncontrollably, his tiny body twisting in Tyson's arms as he tried to escape the tickling.

He started out of the den, Hanes securely in his arms, but couldn't resist throwing a look over his shoulder at Olivia. She had returned her attention to the box, pulling out what looked like a journal, her expression again private and contemplative.

What have I gotten myself into? Olivia was connected to his investigation, possibly even a key to it. He couldn't afford distractions, couldn't allow personal feelings to cloud his judgment. And yet, as he carried Hanes away, he knew with unwelcome certainty that something had shifted between them, something that wouldn't be easily dismissed. Or forgotten.

OLIVIA PAUSED IN the bedroom doorway, her fingers wrapped around a tall glass of water. The night view through the bay window pulled her gaze like a magnet. Dark lake water stretched toward the opposite shore, pinpricks of light from distant homes dancing on the gentle waves. Her chest loosened at the sight, a knot of tension she hadn't realized she'd been carrying until this moment of quiet beauty.

She padded across the bedroom's wood floor in her pajamas, the soft cotton brushing against her skin with each step. The luxurious rental house had exceeded her expectations in every way, but this view, that was what she was paying for. Worth every penny.

In DC, night never truly arrived. Streetlights, headlights, office buildings running skeleton crews. There was always illumination pushing back against the darkness. Here, the darkness had substance. It pooled between the light sources, deep and velvety, making the stars overhead seem impossibly bright and close.

The lake itself was a shifting black mirror broken only by ripples that caught and stretched the reflections. She traced one such ripple with her eyes as it traveled toward the dock that extended from the property into the water. Her gaze lingered on the motorboat tied there, rocking gently with the water's movement.

The boat. She'd almost forgotten about it. The rental agent had mentioned it when handing over the keys, something about it being included with the rental. This time in Galesburg was likely to be as close as she got to an earned vacation this year. She should do one relaxing, vacation-like thing at least. She wondered what it would be like to take it out for a leisurely ride. She'd never piloted a boat before. Was it difficult? Did she need a license?

She turned from the window, her attention shifting to the cardboard box sitting on the bed. The box that contained the fragments of the life of a woman who had given birth to her. Time to see what other secrets they might hold.

She sat cross-legged on the bed, the cardboard box between her knees, methodically exploring each item as if excavating an archaeological site.

She squeezed it, the Care Bear, Harmony Bear. She'd looked up its name on the internet. The stuffing compressed and then slowly expanded again, like the toy was taking a breath. She held it against her chest for a moment, wondering if Annalise had done the same, if this teddy bear had absorbed her birth mother's tears or witnessed her secrets. The bear's plastic eyes reflected nothing back.

She set the bear aside gently, propping it against her pillow where it sat with a slight forward tilt, as if curious about what else the box contained.

The drawing pad was next, its spiral binding worn at the edges. She flipped through a few pages, finding pencil sketches. A tree bent by wind. A face with features only half-defined. A hand reaching just beyond the page's edge. Annalise had talent, that much was clear. Not just technical skill but an ability to capture emotion with minimal lines. She traced one drawing with her fingertip, careful not to smudge the graphite. How strange to share this gift with someone whose blood ran in her veins but whose voice she'd never heard.

Beneath the sketchbook lay a rolled fabric pencil case, secured with a frayed ribbon. She untied it carefully, spreading the fabric flat across the bedspread. Twenty-four slots, each holding a colored pencil. These weren't children's supplies but professional-grade tools, Prismacolor, their labels worn but still legible. She lifted one, testing its weight in her hand. The wood was smooth, polished by years of use. The lead inside had been sharpened to a perfect point and then preserved, as if Annalise had prepared them for their next use. A use that never came.

Olivia's throat tightened. These weren't just art supplies; they were investments. How had a teenage girl afforded them? A birthday gift? Or maybe a gift from her married lover, who could no doubt afford them easily. The care with which they'd been maintained spoke of their value to Annalise.

"So many dreams cut short." she whispered to the empty room. A future Annalise had planned but that had been interrupted by pregnancy. By her.

Running her fingertip along the row of pencils, she made a silent promise. She would use these, but only for special pieces. Important work. They would not be wasted or forgotten again.

At the bottom of the box, beneath tissue paper that crackled beneath her touch, was a hardcover book with embossed lettering. "Galesburg High School, 1994." Annalise's senior year.

The binding creaked as she opened it. She turned pages slowly, skimming past the principal's message and faculty photos, searching for traces of her birth mother. The first mention came in a section labeled Clubs & Activities. There was Annalise listed as an Art Club member. Another page showed her on the school newspaper staff. The homecoming committee included her name among six others.

She paused at a full-page spread showcasing school spirit week. In the center, a large paper tiger, the school mascot, dominated the hallway. Beside it stood Annalise, paintbrush in hand, grinning with unmistakable pride. She couldn't help but be struck by how closely she resembled Annalise. They looked to be about the same height, with the same hazel eyes and light brown hair. Her face was fuller, her nose flatter, but there was no denying the resemblance. She stared at her mother, her birth mother, for several more long moments, memorizing the lines of her face. She'd spent years imagining what Annalise might look like, constructing and reconstructing a face from the few details she knew.

She glanced at the other girl in the photo, who had her arm slung around Annalise. The girl was of similar height to Annalise, but where Annalise's skin was a caramel brown, the other girl's was nearly bone white, set off by teased, fire engine red hair. Their heads tilted together in the easy intimacy of teenage friendship. The caption read: Annalise Lowell and Sarah Garrett put finishing touches on the spirit week tiger.

She continued flipping through the yearbook, past activity pages and candid shots of teenagers frozen in moments of mid-nineties fashion and exuberance.

She reached the senior portraits section, the faces looking back at her, each one in a formal pose against the same mottled blue background. Girls with carefully styled hair. Boys in ties and button-downs. But unlike Olivia's own senior yearbook from her DC high school, where over two hundred graduates had filled page after page of alphabetically arranged portraits, Annalise's graduating class barely covered two pages.

"Thirty-two students." Olivia counted. "The entire graduating class." It was difficult to imagine such a small community. In a class that size, everyone would know everyone—their habits, their families, their secrets. Her own high school experience had been marked by anonymity, the freedom to blend into crowds. Would Annalise have found that smaller environment comforting or suffocating?

She located Annalise's portrait among the *F* surnames, then turned to the *G* section. Annalise had gotten everyone to sign beneath their photo in the yearbook. Unlike many of the formal, stiff poses around her, Sarah looked directly into the camera with a hint of mischief in her expression. Beneath Sarah's portrait was a message written in looping script. "We did it! Can't wait for what the future holds but I know you'll be right there with me. BFF. Love you! S.G."

BFF. Best friends forever. Best friends traded dreams. Confided fears. Shared secrets. If anyone knew the identity of her father, wouldn't it be Annalise's BFF? Had Sarah stood by Annalise when she discovered her pregnancy? Had she known the father? Olivia's pulse quickened as possibilities unfurled. Maybe Sarah Garrett still lived in Galesburg. Maybe she held the answers she had been seeking.

She carefully closed the yearbook, her mind racing. The night had grown late without her noticing, the lights across the lake fewer now as households settled into sleep. But she felt more awake than she had in days, energized by the tangible connection to her past and the potential path forward.

She looked at the scattered items around her. The Care Bear, the art supplies, the yearbook. Fragments that, together, sketched the outline of a young woman with artistic talent, school spirit and at least one close friendship.

She set the yearbook gently on the bedspread and reached for her tablet on the nightstand. The screen illuminated with blue-white light as she opened the browser.

"Sarah Garrett, Galesburg," she typed, her fingers hovering for a moment before tapping the search icon.

There was no guarantee Sarah still lived in town. Three decades had passed, plenty of time for someone to move away. Change their name through marriage, or pass away. But small towns sometimes held people, wrapped them in the familiarity of routine and connection until leaving seemed impossible. Her mind flitted to Tyson. The search results populated her screen before her thoughts could move any further than the memory of his face.

She scrolled past social media hits. Too many Sarah Garretts to bother there. Halfway down the page, an entry caught her attention. Sarah Garrett, Galesburg Family Therapy Services.

She tapped the link, holding her breath as the page loaded. A professional website appeared, cream-colored background with soothing blue accents. "Providing compassionate therapy services to individuals, couples and families in Galesburg for over twenty years," the tagline read. She clicked on the "About" tab and found herself looking at a professional headshot of a woman in her late forties. The teased hair replaced by a shoulder-length bob in a more muted red color. The face had matured, fine lines appearing around the eyes and mouth. But the direct gaze remained, the hint of mischief mixed with confidence. It was Sarah Garrett from the yearbook, aged by thirty years, but unmistakably Annalise's best friend.

Her eyes skimmed the professional biography. A master's degree in family therapy, specialized training in trauma and grief counseling. Extensive community involvement and a personal statement about the healing power of connection. She found the contact information for an office address on Ellis Street and a phone number with the local area code.

She set the tablet on her lap, her mind racing ahead to tomorrow. She planned to pay a visit to Sarah Garrett first thing in the morning. Would it be better to call ahead or simply appear? A call might give Sarah time to refuse the meeting. Showing up might seem rude, but it offered the chance to see Sarah's unfiltered reaction to her appearance and questions.

Olivia picked up her water glass, now warm and half empty, and took a sip. The digital clock on the nightstand showed 12:17 a.m. Too late to do anything except sleep and wait for morning. But she also knew that the energy humming through her veins would likely make sleep impossible.

Hope spread through her chest, tentative but undeniable. Tomorrow, she would meet her mother's best friend and maybe, finally, uncover the truth she'd been seeking.

Chapter Nine

Tyson eased his foot off the gas pedal as he pulled into the driveway of Olivia's rental house, gravel crunching beneath his tires. His knuckles whitened against the steering wheel as he brought the cruiser to a stop. Two cups of coffee, both black, were nestled in the vehicle's cupholders, but he'd gotten cream and sugar since he wasn't sure how Olivia took her coffee.

This is a terrible idea. He pushed the thought aside and cut the engine.

He checked his reflection in the rearview mirror, straightening the collar of his uniform and running a hand over his short-cropped hair, before he grabbed both coffee cups and climbed out of the cruiser.

The three wooden steps to the porch creaked beneath his weight. He shifted both coffee cups to one hand, balancing them carefully as he pressed the doorbell with his free thumb. The chime echoed inside, followed by footsteps.

His pulse quickened. He straightened his shoulders, adopting what he hoped was a pleasant, open smile. The lock clicked, and the front door swung open.

Olivia stood in the doorway, her hair pulled back in a loose ponytail, wearing jeans and a simple gray T-shirt, and she was barefoot. Her expression wasn't as surprised as he would have expected.

"I brought coffee," he said, lifting the cups as if she might not have noticed them.

She studied him for a moment, then she stepped aside. The scent of her shampoo, floral and subtle, drifted past him as he entered, careful not to brush against her in the narrow entryway.

"Kitchen's this way," she said, her voice soft but steady as she led him toward the rear of the house.

He followed, taking in the details of her temporary home. A laptop open on the coffee table. Books piled haphazardly on the single bookshelf. No photos, no personal touches. Nothing to tie her to this place or to anyone else.

The kitchen was large with bright, morning light streaming through windows that overlooked the backyard, dock and lake. She stopped at the island counter and turned to face him, arms crossed loosely over her chest. Not defensive, exactly, but not entirely open either.

He extended one of the cups toward her. "I wasn't sure how you take it, so I brought cream and sugar packets." He patted his pants pocket where he'd stashed several.

Her fingers brushed his as she accepted the cup. The contact sent a shock of attraction through him. She cradled the cup between her palms, not drinking, just holding it like it might warm her from the outside in.

"To what do I owe this visit?" Her tone was neutral, careful.

He leaned against the counter, giving her space. "I just wanted to check on you after last night." He took a sip of his coffee, using the moment to gather his thoughts. "Family dinner and the box of items from Annalise, that was a lot to deal with at once."

The corner of her mouth twitched, her gaze slipping away from his, focusing instead on the lid of her coffee cup. Her fingernail picked at the plastic as if trying to pry loose a secret.

"I'm fine," she said. "Thank you for your concern."

The words were polite the kind people used when they wanted to end conversations about feelings before they began. He recognized the deflection.

He took another sip of his coffee, the bitter liquid warming his throat. "You know," he said, keeping his voice gentle, "fine is not a feeling."

Her eyes snapped back to his, surprise flickering across her face before she could mask it. The coffee cup in her hands tilted, and she quickly righted it, a faint flush creeping up her neck.

For a moment, he thought she might tell him to leave and mind his own business. Instead, her expression shifted. Vulnerability.

But that wasn't why he was here. Not really. He was the police chief, not a friend, not a confidant. He was here because he had a job to do, a case to investigate, even if that case was decades old and cold as the grave.

And yet, watching her finger trace the rim of the coffee cup, he couldn't deny the pull he felt toward this woman who'd suddenly appeared in his town looking for answers about a mother she'd never known.

Olivia set the coffee cup on the island counter. Her shoulders rose and fell with a deep breath, her expression a complicated mix of frustration and vulnerability that made his chest tighten. "I don't know how I feel," she admitted. "I went through the box that Stephanie gave me last night. Annalise's yearbook was in there." Her gaze went unfocused as if she was looking somewhere beyond the kitchen walls. "Looking at it was like a window into her life, but—" she threw up her hands "—I don't know if it even matters. Annalise is gone, my adoptive mother is gone. I have no one."

The raw honesty in her voice caught him off guard.

He set down his own coffee and moved closer, not crowding her but closing enough of the distance that she could sense his presence as more than just professional. The morning sunlight pouring through the window caught the flecks of gold in her eyes, making them appear almost amber.

"I'm sure that's not true," he said softly.

She looked up at him, her expression speaking volumes more than words. He could read it as clear as if she'd shouted it. You don't even know me. The unspoken challenge hung between them, and he realized with startling clarity that he wanted to. He wanted to know everything about her, not just as the police chief investigating her mother's unsolved murder case, but as a man who found himself increasingly drawn to a woman who walked through the world carrying too much on her shoulders.

He glanced at her untouched coffee cup, searching for neutral ground. "Your coffee is going to get cold."

A faint blush colored Olivia's cheeks as she looked away. "I don't drink coffee."

The admission caught him off guard, making him feel foolish for his presumption. "Oh, sorry," he managed to say, shoving his hands behind his back to keep from fidgeting like a teenager.

Olivia's expression softened unexpectedly, the corners of her mouth lifting in a smile that transformed her face. "No. It was a nice gesture."

Something electric passed between them in that moment. A current of attraction neither had acknowledged but both could feel. He noticed the curve of her neck, the way a strand of hair had escaped her ponytail to brush against her cheek. His fingers itched with the impulse to tuck it back, but it was an intimacy he had no right to.

He cleared his throat, taking a half step back. "I don't want to take up your morning."

His professional mask slipped back into place as he straightened his shoulders, feeling the weight of his badge against his chest. This wasn't a social call, no matter how much a part of him wished it could be. He was the police chief first, and whatever this pull toward Olivia might be, it had to come second.

"I'm actually here to let you know that I will be taking a fresh look at Annalise's hit-and-run case."

"Thank you," she breathed, hope blooming across her face.

"It's not a favor," he said, though the gratitude in her eyes made his chest warm in a way he tried to ignore. "Someone is responsible for Annalise's death, one way or another, and they should be held responsible. It might help if I could take a look at the items in that box Stephanie gave you last night."

She hesitated, the reluctance in her eyes telling him how precious the items already were to her.

"I know those things are probably important to you," he added. "But they might lead to witnesses I should speak to or even a suspect."

Her fingers drummed lightly on the counter before she nodded. "Yes, of course. Whatever you need." She hesitated again. "There was a yearbook in the box, and it seems like Annalise was close with another girl named Sarah Garrett." Her voice gained confidence as she continued, leaning forward. "I looked her up online last night, and Sarah Garrett is now a therapist in town."

His lips curved into a knowing smile. Under different circumstances, he might have lectured her about civilians conducting their own investigations, but he couldn't muster any real disapproval. In her position, he'd have done the same thing. "Let me guess," he said. "You plan to try and speak to Sarah Garrett."

Her lips stretched into a grin that transformed her entire face. The guarded woman who'd opened the door to him minutes ago vanished, replaced by someone whose hope shimmered almost tangibly in the sunlit kitchen. The change was so striking that he went momentarily speechless, his heart thudding against his ribs with unexpected force.

"I may have had a visit to her office on my to-do list for the day," she admitted.

"How would you feel about us going together?" The words left his mouth before he could second-guess them.

Surprise flickered across her face, her eyes widening. "Really?"

He noticed details he had no business focusing on, the curve of her collarbone, the small scar near her left eyebrow and the way her fingers curled over the edge of the counter as she awaited his response.

"Really," he confirmed, shifting back into professional mode even as something more personal tugged at him. "Having me with you will at least get you in to see Sarah without an appointment." He leaned against the granite island, careful to maintain an appropriate distance. "And I can vouch for you being Annalise's daughter since most people in town aren't likely to be excited about talking to an outsider about the past."

Her expression changed, latching on to his words with an intensity that made him realize what he'd said. "So, you do believe I am Annalise's daughter."

He nodded without hesitation. In his thirteen years in law enforcement, he'd learned to trust his instincts about people. It wasn't just her physical resemblance to Annalise.

"I do," he said simply. "But Stephanie told me you two took a DNA test. That will go a long way to put any questions to rest."

The relief that washed over her face was palpable. Her

shoulders relaxed, releasing tension he hadn't fully registered until it disappeared.

Her smile grew even wider, revealing a dimple in her right cheek that Tyson hadn't noticed before. His heart performed another unexpected stutter step.

"We can stop by UPS so I can send the test kit before we go to see Sarah," she said, animated by a hope that seemed to brighten the entire kitchen.

He returned her smile, aware of the shift between them. He was stepping beyond the boundaries he usually maintained so carefully, becoming involved in a way that went beyond duty. He should probably be more cautious, more reserved.

Instead, he said, "I'll drive."

Chapter Ten

Olivia's heart hammered against her ribs as she followed Tyson into Sarah Garrett's office. This was a chance to speak with someone who might hold the key to unlocking the mystery of her birth father's identity.

The therapy office's reception area smelled of lemon polish and was unexpectedly homey for a professional space. Fresh flowers sat on the receptionist's desk, and a soft, fabric sofa enticed patients to sit and wait. Olivia smoothed her hands down her pants, fighting the urge to fidget.

"Chief, it's a surprise to see you here," Sarah said, leading them out of her reception area just as the phone rang. The sound faded as they moved deeper into the private office, the thick carpet muffling their footsteps.

"I'm sorry for dropping in on you like this, Sarah, but it is important. Let me introduce Olivia Lowell." Tyson's voice carried the easy authority Olivia had come to recognize as his professional tone.

Sarah turned toward Olivia, hand extended, confusion still evident in the slight furrow between her brows. Olivia accepted the handshake, noting the firm grip and smooth, cool skin. She searched Sarah's face for any sign of recognition that might tell her Sarah had the answers she sought.

Sarah was a tall woman, with soft curves and bright blue eyes and red hair shot through with gray. Lines around her eyes and mouth showed her age but also testified to a life of smiles and laughter. She waved them toward a seating area in the corner of her office, two armchairs and a sofa arranged around a low table. "What can I do for you, Chief?"

Olivia looked at Tyson, letting him take the lead. He was the police officer, and if he was really reopening Annalise's case, his questions would likely be similar to hers and more important. He could soften Sarah up first, and she could jump in when the time was right.

"Well, we were hoping to talk to you about Annalise Farr," Tyson said. "It's my understanding that you and she were rather close in high school."

Sarah leaned back in her chair, letting out a little breath of air with a woosh. Her surprise seemed genuine. Sarah couldn't have expected Tyson to come asking about Annalise after all these years.

"We were," Sarah confirmed. "But that was a long time ago. Why are you asking about…" Her voice trailed off as she looked at Olivia again, studying her more intently. Then another gasp escaped Sarah's lips.

"You're…" Sarah said, the word hanging in the air like a promise.

Sarah laughed, a nervous sound that seemed to catch in her throat. Sarah recognized her. Sarah knew who she was. The realization sent electricity dancing across her skin.

"No one. You…you just look like someone I knew, but you can't be."

"I can't be Annalise's daughter?" Olivia pressed. "I am. I'm the child that Annalise gave away for adoption."

The declaration hung in the air. Olivia watched Sarah's face, hungry for her reaction.

Sarah leaned back farther into the sofa. "No…you…you can't be."

Was Sarah afraid of something? Hiding something? Olivia shifted in her seat, ready to demand the truth that had been withheld from her for three decades.

Tyson jumped into the conversation before she could press further, his calm voice cutting through the tension like a knife through butter. "Sarah, would you mind answering some questions about Annalise?" The shift in his tone was subtle but effective.

"Yes, of course." Sarah visibly pulled herself together, running her hand over the front of her suit jacket and straightening her back. "Although I'm not sure how much help I can be. Annalise and I were best friends in high school, but she passed away tragically, thirty years ago."

"Yes, ma'am, I know," Tyson said, nodding. "In a hit-and-run on Route 360. It's still an open case, and I've decided it's high time to take another look at it."

Sarah's eyes widened, the blue irises brightening against suddenly pale skin. "Well, I certainly want to help you however I can. The accident was tragic, and it has never sat well with me that no one took responsibility for it."

Olivia noticed that Sarah's eyes kept darting between her and Tyson, as if she couldn't take her eyes off her. Sarah seemed both drawn to and unsettled by her presence, almost as if she'd encountered a ghost.

"Do you have any idea why Annalise was on Route 360 the night she was killed?" Tyson asked, his voice casual but his eyes sharp.

Sarah looked a little surprised by the question, her eyebrows lifting. Olivia leaned forward, not wanting to miss any nuance of Sarah's response.

"It's not exactly on the route to her parents' home, where she was living at the time. And it was late," Tyson continued, pulling a notepad from his front pocket and flipping to a clean page.

"No," Sarah said, shaking her head. "I've wondered that myself, but I have no idea."

Olivia studied Sarah's face, noting the tight line of Sarah's mouth, the way her fingers curled and uncurled against her thigh.

"Annalise was found at approximately 3:00 a.m. by a man rushing his pregnant wife to the hospital. Do you know if Annalise knew anyone who lived out that way at that time?" Tyson cleared his throat. "Maybe she was visiting someone?"

A veil fell over Sarah's eyes. She was clamming up.

"It's possible, I suppose," Sarah said in a measured tone. "But I have no idea who it could have been."

Liar, Olivia thought, the word flashing through her mind. Sarah's careful composure, the way she avoided direct eye contact with her or Tyson. It all screamed deception. But why would she lie? What was she hiding after all these years? Who was she protecting? Herself or someone else?

"Annalise confide in you when she got pregnant?" Tyson continued, shifting tactics smoothly.

Sarah hesitated for a moment then nodded. "Right after she found out. She swore me to secrecy."

Olivia slid to the end of the chair, excitement coursing through her veins. Here it was—confirmation that Sarah had known about her existence. She started to speak, a dozen questions crowding her throat, but Tyson cut her off with a look.

"Had you known about her relationship with the father prior to her telling you about the pregnancy?" Tyson asked, his tone conversational but persistent.

Olivia forced herself to breathe evenly, to appear calm while her mind raced. Sarah had known Annalise was pregnant. Sarah had been sworn to secrecy. Which meant Sarah might know who her father was.

"I did. Not at first," Sarah hurriedly added, "but after a while it became clear that something was going on."

Tyson seemed to catch on Sarah's words, his head tilting. "How did it become clear?"

Sarah shrugged. "Annalise didn't want to hang out as much, but she'd ask me to cover for her if her parents asked if she'd been with me." A ghost of a smile touched Sarah's lips. "When she finally told me she was seeing someone, it was kind of exciting. A secret romance."

The smile faded, replaced by a frown that deepened the lines around Sarah's mouth. "Or at least that's how it felt at nineteen."

Olivia watched the play of emotions across Sarah's face, searching for tells, for signs of deception, but found none.

"How long did the secret romance go on?" Tyson asked.

Sarah looked up at the ceiling as if she was trying to recall, her eyes tracing the pattern of recessed lighting. "A year, give or take, I think, before Annalise told me she was pregnant."

A year. Olivia did the mental calculation. If Annalise had been seeing someone for a year before discovering her pregnancy, then this wasn't some casual fling or one-night stand. This was a relationship. Something serious enough to maintain in secret for months on end.

Tyson looked at Olivia now, a subtle nod indicating it was her turn. Her heart rate quickened as she seized the opening.

"Do you know who fathered Annalise's child?" Olivia asked.

Sarah hesitated, her gaze fixed somewhere over Olivia's shoulder. "No. I'm sorry. Annalise never told me his name."

Sarah was clearly not telling them everything. "You didn't

have any idea?" she pressed, leaning forward, the coffee table digging into her shins, but she barely noticed.

"No." Sarah's response was clipped, and she wouldn't look directly at her.

Olivia's back stiffened. "I find it hard to believe you were Annalise's best friend, the person she trusted to cover for her," she said, using Sarah's own words as ammunition, "and she didn't tell you anything at all about her secret lover."

Sarah looked her in the eyes now, fire in her eyes. "I don't know what to tell you. She didn't tell me who she was seeing."

Another lie. Olivia was certain of it.

Sarah rose abruptly. "I'm sorry. I have a patient coming soon. I wish I could have been more help."

Olivia remained seated, her body a statement of defiance. She opened her mouth to press Sarah further, determined not to let this opportunity slip away. Before she could speak, Tyson stood up, gently pulling her up with him.

"Please call if you think of anything else that might help," Tyson said, taking a business card from his shirt pocket and handing it to Sarah.

She wanted to protest, to dig in her heels and demand answers, but Tyson shifted so that she was in front of him. She felt him at her back, as he guided her forward and out of the office.

Frustration built inside her with each step away from Sarah, away from answers. They moved through the reception area and out of the building. She contained her fury until they reached the sidewalk in front of the building, the spring air doing nothing to cool the heat of her indignation.

She whirled on Tyson, her hands clenched into tight fists at her sides. "What was that?" she demanded, her voice low but vibrating with intensity. The frustration she'd been bottling up now threatened to overflow.

"That was me doing my job," Tyson replied, his tone maddeningly calm. He stood with his hands at his side, unruffled by her outburst.

"Your job?" Her voice rose despite her effort to control it. A woman passing by glanced their way, then quickened her pace. "Is your job to let her get away with not telling us everything she knows? Because she definitely knows more than what she told us."

Tyson tapped his temple and sighed, a gesture that made her want to scream. How could he be so composed when they'd just wasted their best opportunity to learn the truth?

"I know that," he said, "but pushing her wasn't going to get her to tell us. This work takes time. To build trust. To get people comfortable opening up about secrets they've held on to for years, decades in this case. You can't expect answers right away."

She scoffed. "Right away? It's been thirty years. She's had thirty years to get comfortable telling the truth, and that hasn't done it. I think it's time she's forced to open up."

She started back toward the building, determination hardening her resolve.

Tyson maneuvered so his large body blocked her path. "Olivia, listen to me." His voice was soft, but firm. "If you go back in there guns blazing, I'll have to trespass you from the premises. Sarah could seek a restraining order, and then you might never get to speak to her again. Is that what you want?"

She gritted her teeth, frustration warring with the rational part of her mind that recognized the truth in his words. "No, of course not," she admitted reluctantly.

Tyson put his hands on her shoulders, and a jolt shot through her at his touch. The warmth of his palms seemed to burn through the fabric of her blouse. "Then trust me, please," he said, his eyes holding hers. "Give Sarah some time to think about our discussion. Then we'll reach out to her again. In my experience, we will get more out of her. We just have to be patient."

She growled, a low sound of frustration. Patient. She'd been patient for thirty years. Had waited through childhood wondering why her birth mother had given her up. Through adolescence searching for her features in every woman who passed. And now, to be so close.

As if he could read her thoughts, he said, "A few more days, that's all it might take."

Every bone in her body was telling her to go back into Sarah's office and demand the answers she was entitled to. *Trust me.* The words echoed in her mind, setting off a cascade of doubt. The only person she'd ever truly trusted was her adoptive mother. But she was gone now, and she was alone in a town where she barely knew anyone, where no one really wanted her there. At least Tyson was willing to help her. She might not be able to trust him fully, but she could trust him with this, at least for now.

She let out a deep breath, her shoulders slumping under his large hands. "Okay. We'll play it your way."

For now, she added silently.

He gave her a crooked smile, almost as if he'd heard the words she didn't say. She wondered how a man who didn't know her could seemingly read her so well, but the answer that flitted across her mind was scary.

She was thankful when her phone beeped with an incoming email, providing a welcome distraction.

She pulled her phone out, the screen bright in the midday sun. She squinted as she opened the notification, her heart leaping at the message from the lawyer she'd hired to help get her adoption file unsealed.

Tyson dropped his hands from her shoulders, taking a step back. “Good news?”

She looked up from the phone, the frustration that had been churning inside her moments before transformed into a rush of excitement. “Great news. My adoption case has been unsealed.”

Chapter Eleven

The sidewalk outside the therapist's office buzzed with midmorning activity, but Tyson focused solely on the cell phone in Olivia's hand. He positioned himself just behind her right shoulder, close enough to see the screen but not so close that she'd feel crowded. The faint scent of her perfume drifted up to him, and he fought to keep his mind on the task at hand.

"It's downloading now," Olivia said, her finger tapping impatiently against the side of her phone. "The attachment was larger than I expected."

He nodded, though she couldn't see him. The sun cast a halo around her hair, highlighting the subtle auburn undertones he'd never noticed before. She wore it pulled back today, exposing the gentle curve of her neck. He swallowed and looked away, scanning the street for a moment to clear his head.

When he looked back, she had opened the file, tilting the phone as if inviting him to see better. He leaned in, his chest nearly touching her back. He could feel the warmth radiating from her body through the thin fabric of her blouse. If he moved just an inch closer…

"I hate these little screens," he said. The text on the phone was tiny.

Olivia glanced over her shoulder at his comment, and suddenly they were face-to-face, her eyes wide and questioning. He found himself unable to look away. He could see the faint freckles across the bridge of her nose, almost invisible against her skin. Her lips parted, and for one charged moment, the adoption paperwork seemed to evaporate from both their minds.

She turned away abruptly, her shoulders tensing. "I can pull it up on my tablet. It's in my purse," she said, her hand already reaching for the bag slung over her shoulder.

"No. This is fine." His voice a rumble. He cleared his throat, hoping she hadn't noticed the change in his tone. *Get it together, Tyson. This is about her search, not your misplaced attraction.*

Olivia returned her attention to the phone. Her fingers gripped the device a little tighter than necessary. Was she affected by his proximity too? He pushed the thought aside, forcing himself to concentrate on the document.

"There's not much here," she said after a moment, scrolling slowly through the text. "There's no father's name listed." Defeat laced her words.

He peered at the screen, pointing to a line near the bottom of the page. "It says the father is unknown or can't be located." His finger brushed against hers for a split second, and he withdrew it quickly. "I bet whoever helped Annalise with the adoption made sure that she didn't offer up the father's name."

She nodded, her eyes still fixed on the screen. "Yeah, Amelia said she thought the father of Annalise's baby paid for her to go to New York. He probably paid for the adoption too, to make sure his name remained a secret."

Her thumb moved across the screen as she scrolled down farther, stopping when she reached a signature at the bottom of the document. "'Waldo Emerson,'" she read aloud.

"Waldo Emerson," he repeated. The name rang a distant bell in his memory.

Olivia whipped around to face him again, this time all business, the earlier moment of tension forgotten. "You know him?" Her eyes were bright with hope.

"There's a law firm named Emerson & Associates just outside of Montville," he explained, recalling the brick building he'd passed countless times on the drive to the county courthouse. "I'm not sure if there's any connection, but it's worth looking into."

"Can we go now?"

He gave her a measured look, one eyebrow raised.

"I promise to behave," she added, reading his expression. "But this lawyer, if my birth father paid for his services, Waldo Emerson has to know who he is."

He sighed, running a hand over his hair. "He may not be able to give us an answer. If your birth father did pay for his services, he may be bound by attorney-client privilege."

Her face fell, the hope in her eyes dimming. Something tightened in his chest at the sight. She'd had been through so much already in her search, each lead ending in disappointment or more questions. He could see her mind working, processing the implications of what he'd said. Being so close to an answer, knowing someone might have the information she desperately wanted but couldn't or wouldn't share it was its own kind of torture.

"I'll take that chance," she said, her jaw set with determination.

Tyson studied her face for a moment longer. She would go with or without him, and at least if he went along, he could keep her from doing something they'd both regret later.

"Okay," he conceded. "Let's go talk to a lawyer."

Relief washed over her face, followed by a smile that made his heart stutter in his chest. She slipped her phone back into her purse and started toward his car. He followed a few paces behind, trying to ignore the way his body still hummed from their brief proximity. He was a professional, here to help Olivia find answers about her past and find the person responsible for Annalise's death. Nothing more. He repeated this to himself as he unlocked the car doors, hoping that if he thought it enough times, he might actually start to believe it.

THE DRIVE TO Montville took twenty-five minutes, though Tyson suspected it felt like much longer to Olivia. She sat in the passenger seat of his department-issued SUV, too wound up to engage in any real conversation. Her fingers drummed against her thigh, and every few minutes she checked her phone as if expecting the adoption papers to somehow reveal new information. He kept his eyes on the road, giving her space. After months of waiting for her lawyer to get the adoption papers unsealed, he understood why she was on edge.

The name on those adoption papers represented the first concrete lead they'd had. But he had encountered enough dead ends in his career to know that promising trails often led nowhere. He glanced at Olivia, noting the tight line of her jaw and the way she stared through the windshield without really seeing the landscape. He didn't have the heart to dampen her hope, but he worried about how she would handle another possible disappointment.

Emerson & Associates occupied the first floor of a modest two-story brick building. The parking lot held about a dozen cars. He pulled into an empty space near the entrance and cut the engine. They exited the car and went into the building, passing through the scant security and taking the elevator to the second floor where Emerson & Associates had their offices.

The reception area greeted them with plush carpeting in a subdued beige, leather chairs arranged in a semicircle. A glass partition separated the waiting area from what appeared to be the main workspace. Through the glass partition, Tyson could make out a series of cubicles likely occupied by paralegals or assistants. Closed doors lined the walls, the private offices of the attorneys. The setup spoke of a well-established firm that was outwardly successful.

"Ready?" he asked.

Olivia nodded, a quick jerk of her head that betrayed her nerves. "As I'll ever be."

The receptionist sat behind a curved desk of polished maple, a middle-aged woman with reading glasses perched on the end of her nose and fingernails the color of dried blood. She looked up from her computer screen with the practiced smile of someone who had mastered the art of professional distance.

He approached, offering a smile that he knew from experience struck the right balance between friendly and authoritative. "Good morning. We're here to see Waldo Emerson."

"Do you have an appointment?" Her fingers hovered over her keyboard, ready to confirm or deny their existence in the day's schedule.

"No, ma'am." Tyson reached into his pocket and produced his badge, holding it where she could see it without making a show for anyone else in the waiting area. "Chief Tyson Morrow, Galesburg PD. This is Olivia Lowell. We'd like to speak with Mr. Waldo Emerson. It won't take much of his time."

The receptionist's eyes widened at the sight of the badge. He watched her internal calculation, weighing the lack of appointment against the potential importance of a police chief's visit.

"May I ask what this is regarding?" Her voice had taken on that particular tone people used when they were trying to be helpful without overstepping their authority.

"Something we're hoping Mr. Emerson can help us with," Tyson said with a closed off smile.

The receptionist hesitated only a moment before lifting the receiver of her phone. "One moment, please." She pressed a button and turned away, speaking in low tones. "Mr. Emerson, there's a Chief Tyson Morrow from Galesburg Police Department here to see you, along with a woman… Yes… He won't say… Of course, sir."

She replaced the receiver and gestured toward a seating area. "Mr. Emerson will be with you shortly. Please, make yourselves comfortable."

"Thank you," he said, guiding Olivia toward the chairs with a light touch on her elbow.

They sat side by side, Olivia perched on the edge of her seat while he leaned back, crossing one leg over the other in a deliberate show of relaxation he didn't feel. The magazines were arranged in a perfect fan on the table in front of the sofa, their glossy covers reflecting the recessed lighting above. Tyson picked one up, pretending to browse while observing Olivia from the corner of his eye.

"Ten minutes," he said quietly. "If they make us wait longer than that, it means they're either genuinely busy or deliberately trying to establish dominance."

Olivia glanced at him, surprise briefly replacing anxiety on her face. "Is that a cop thing, analyzing wait times?"

"More of a human nature thing," he replied, smiling. "But yes, the job makes you pay attention to patterns."

The minutes stretched. He watched the minute hand on his watch complete one full rotation, then another. Around them, the office hummed with quiet efficiency, phones ringing, the soft tap of keyboards, hushed conversations.

Olivia's fingers drummed against her thigh.

At the nine-minute mark, a man emerged through a set of

glass doors at the far end of the reception area. Tyson assessed Waldo Emerson. Mid-forties, a few inches under six feet tall, neatly combed dark hair with the first hints of gray at the temples, clean-shaven, and wearing a suit that Tyson could tell was expensive. The man moved with the easy confidence of someone who had never questioned his place in the world.

He approached them with a practiced smile. “Chief Morrow? Ms. Lowell? I’m Waldo Emerson. Sorry to keep you waiting.”

Tyson stood, accepting the extended hand and noting the flashy watch that peeked from beneath the cuff of Emerson’s shirt.

“Thank you for seeing us without an appointment,” Tyson said. “I appreciate you making the time.”

“Of course. We always cooperate with law enforcement.” Emerson turned to Olivia, who had risen from her chair. “Ms. Lowell, pleased to meet you.”

He caught the flash of confusion that crossed Olivia’s face. This Waldo Emerson was only a decade or so older than he and Olivia. Far too young to have handled an adoption over thirty years ago. He kept his expression neutral, though internally he was already reassessing their approach.

“It’s Olivia, please,” she said, shaking the man’s hand. “Thank you for seeing us.”

Emerson nodded, showing no flicker of recognition at her name. “Why don’t we move to one of our conference rooms where we can speak privately? This way, please.”

Tyson walked beside Olivia, close enough to murmur, “Not the same guy.”

“I noticed,” she whispered back, her disappointment evident even in those two words.

The conference room was in keeping with the rest of the firm’s decor. A heavy wooden table that could accommodate twelve butter-soft leather chairs, and the latest presentation technology mounted to the walls and ceiling. Floor-to-ceiling windows offered a view of the city that probably added at least one zero to the monthly rent.

"Please, make yourselves comfortable," Emerson said, gesturing to the chairs. "Can I offer you anything to drink? Water, coffee, tea?"

"No, thank you," Tyson said. Olivia shook her head.

They sat on one side of the table and Emerson sat on the other side.

Emerson folded his hands on the table. "So, what can I help you with today?"

Olivia straightened in her chair. "Mr. Emerson, I'm looking for information about my birth parents. I was adopted as an infant in 1995."

Emerson's expression remained professionally attentive, but he could see no spark of recognition in his eyes.

"I recently learned that my birth mother, Annalise Farr, died shortly after I was born," Olivia continued. "I never knew anything about my biological family until a few months ago when I discovered relatives here in Galesburg."

"I see," Emerson said, his tone measured and sympathetic. "That must have been quite a revelation for you."

"It was," Olivia agreed. "I've connected with some of my mother's family, but no one seems to know who my father is. The only lead I have is your name on the adoption papers as the attorney that handled the case."

"I'm afraid there's been a misunderstanding. The Waldo Emerson on your adoption papers would be my father, Waldo Emerson Sr. He founded this firm forty years ago."

He saw Olivia's posture stiffen, her hope visibly recalibrating. Her knuckles whitened against the dark wood of the table.

"Your father," she repeated.

"Yes." Emerson's expression grew somber. "I'm afraid he passed away two years ago from a heart attack. It was quite sudden."

"I'm sorry for your loss," Tyson offered automatically.

"Thank you," Emerson said.

"Sorry for your loss," Olivia mumbled, though Tyson could hear the disappointment overwhelming her sympathy.

A silence filled the room, thick with Olivia's unasked questions. He broke in. "Mr. Emerson, would your firm still have records of Olivia's case? Even with your father's passing?"

Emerson's fingers tapped lightly against the polished table. "We maintain records, yes, though files from the nineties would be archived. The bigger issue is attorney-client privilege. Even with my father gone, those ethical obligations remain intact."

"But if the client is deceased..." Olivia began.

"The privilege survives the client's death," Emerson explained gently. "It's one of the most fundamental principles of legal ethics."

Tyson had anticipated this response.

"What if the birth father was the actual client?" he suggested. "If he paid for the services?"

"That would only strengthen the confidentiality requirements," Emerson countered. "We would then need consent from both parties involved to release any information."

Olivia's voice took on an edge. "I'm not asking for the whole file. Just a name. That's all I need. Just to know who he is."

Emerson's refusal came wrapped in genuine sympathy, but remained firm. "I understand how important this is to you, truly. But I can't violate the ethics of my profession, even for such a compelling reason. Attorney-client privilege is absolute in these situations."

"Even thirty years later?" Olivia pressed.

"Even then," Emerson confirmed. "There's no statute of limitations on confidentiality."

The moment reminded Tyson of making death notifications to victims' families. No matter how gently delivered, the loss cut deep. He'd seen the same cycle of disbelief, anger and resignation countless times.

"Is there any way we could petition for access?" he asked, knowing the answer.

"You could try to get a court order," Emerson said, "but without compelling legal necessity, which personal genealogical research typically doesn't qualify as, it's unlikely to be granted."

Olivia's shoulders slumped. She looked down at her hands, now twisted together in her lap. "So that's it, then. Another dead end."

"I truly am sorry," Emerson said, and Tyson believed him. "If there was anything I could ethically do to help, I would."

A heavy silence settled over the room. Tyson placed a reassuring hand over Olivia's, feeling the slight tremor in her fingers. The gesture was instinctive, something he might have done for anyone in distress, but the warmth of her skin against his lingered.

"Thank you for your time," he said, rising. Olivia followed his lead, her movements mechanical.

Emerson stood as well. "I wish I could have been more helpful."

They followed Emerson back to the reception area. The receptionist glanced up as they passed, following them with her gaze as Waldo walked them to the doors of the firm. "Again, I'm sorry I couldn't be of more help," Emerson offered, before disappearing through the glass doors he'd come out of earlier.

Tyson watched Olivia's composure crack the moment

Waldo disappeared. Her fingers curled into tight fists at her sides, and a muscle jumped in her jaw. "We have to make him tell us," she said. "My birth father's name has to be in his records. And he could know something about Annalise's death. You need to talk to him about a possible crime. Can't you do anything?"

His gaze flicked to the receptionist, who had suddenly become very interested in her computer screen, though her typing had ceased. The woman's head was tilted in their direction, her earrings catching the light as she strained to hear their conversation while pretending not to. Years of interviewing witnesses had made Tyson acutely aware of when someone was eavesdropping.

"Let's get out of here," he said quietly. He placed his hand lightly on Olivia's elbow and guided her toward the exit, away from the receptionist's curious ears. She and Tyson were both silent until they were outside.

"I could try to subpoena the firm's records," he said, keeping his voice measured despite his frustration. "But that's more than a long shot. The bar for getting a subpoena for attorney records is astronomical, and we are nowhere near meeting it."

Olivia drew a deep breath, visibly calming herself, her shoulders dropping from their tensed position near her ears. "Okay, so now what?" The question was simple, but the weight behind it was anything but.

He considered their options. With regard to finding her birth father's name, it seemed like they were at a dead end. But he still had quite a bit of work to do to see if he could dig up a lead with respect to Annalise's hit-and-run. It was possible, heck even likely, that there was a connection between Annalise giving up her baby and her death. He glanced at Olivia. A connection that she hadn't seemed to make yet. At least not to him. But her birth father was a natural suspect in Annalise's death.

"Now, we keep digging," he said with determination. "Annalise lived here all her life before going to New York for the birth. Someone in town might know something about who she was involved with back then. Even if they don't realize it."

They walked to the SUV and he continued, "There's still the accident that killed Annalise. Maybe reviewing those files could turn up a lead for us to follow."

Olivia nodded. Tyson opened the passenger door for her. She slid onto the seat then looked up at him. "Thank you," she said. "For not giving up."

The words settled somewhere deep in his chest. He closed her door and circled around to the driver's side, using the moment to compose himself. This case was affecting him more than it should, crossing lines he'd always kept firmly drawn between his professional and personal lives. He should step back, create some distance.

Instead, as he got behind the wheel, he was already planning their next steps. The rational part of his mind warned him he was getting too invested. The rest of him didn't seem to care.

"We'll start with the accident reports first thing tomorrow," he said, starting the SUV's engine.

Chapter Twelve

His fingers drummed an irregular rhythm against the polished mahogany of his desk, each tap sending tiny vibrations up his arm. The investigation was progressing faster than he'd anticipated. He swiveled in his leather chair to face the window, where gray clouds hung heavy over the town, mirroring the storm brewing inside him. The warning he'd left on Olivia's door should have sent her running. The message had been clear. Direct enough to frighten, vague enough to avoid specifics. GO HOME. Simple. Effective. Or so he'd thought.

But somehow, that stubborn woman was still here. Still digging. Still threatening everything he'd built.

He pressed his palms flat against the cool surface of the desk, trying to still the tremor that had taken up residence in his hands over the past week, a physical manifestation of the fear that now lived in his gut like a parasite, feeding on his composure bit by bit.

She was supposed to be gone by now. That had been the plan. Scare her enough that she'd retreat to wherever she'd come from, too frightened to even think about Galesburg again. But Olivia had proven herself to be made of sterner stuff than he'd calculated.

He rose from the chair, the leather squeaking as he pushed away from the desk. His home office, once a sanctuary of control and order, now felt like a cage. Certificates and commendations hung on the walls, evidence of a life carefully constructed, brick by meticulous brick.

He paced the length of the room. Nothing about this situation was turning out as planned. Not only was Olivia still here, but now the chief of police was apparently helping her. That particular development sent a fresh surge of acid into his stomach.

"Damn it," he muttered, the words hanging in the quiet of the room.

It should have been so simple. The past should have stayed buried, like all the other secrets in this town. Instead, it was clawing its way to the surface, threatening to drag him down with it.

He paused at the window, looking out at his perfectly manicured lawn. The shrill ring of his cell phone sliced through his thoughts. The screen lit up with a name that made his jaw clench. Waldo Emerson Jr.

His hand closed around the phone, hesitating for just a moment before he swiped to answer. "Hello, Waldo," he said.

"Hey there." Waldo's voice came through, too casual, too familiar. "Got a minute to talk?"

"I'm rather busy at the moment." A lie. He had nowhere to be, nothing to do but pace his office and contemplate the unraveling of his life. "What is it?"

"Thought you should know I had some visitors at the office today. Chief Morrow and that Lowell woman."

His free hand curled into a fist, nails digging half-moons into his palm. He forced himself to breathe evenly, to keep his voice steady. "Is that so? What did they want?"

"They were asking questions about Olivia's adoption. Specifically, about how my father assisted with it."

The room seemed to tilt sideways, the framed accolades on the wall blurring as panic swept through him in a hot wave.

They know. They know. They know.

The words pulsed in his mind in time with his racing heart. If they knew Waldo's father had helped with the adoption, it wouldn't take much more digging to uncover the rest. And then everything, his position, his reputation, his freedom, would be gone.

"What did you tell them?" His voice emerged as a harsh whisper, scraping past the constriction in his throat.

"Relax," Waldo said, and the killer could almost see the dismissive wave of his hand. "I didn't tell them a thing. I hid behind attorney-client privilege. They can't make me talk."

He closed his eyes, relief washing through him. Then Waldo continued, and the relief curdled into something else entirely.

"But, you know, maintaining that kind of discretion is… expensive."

There it was. The real reason for the call. Anger flared hot in his chest, burning away the last vestiges of his panic, replacing it with a cold, clear fury.

"Are you blackmailing me, Waldo?" he asked, his voice dropping to a dangerous register.

"Blackmail is such an ugly word," Waldo replied, a nervous laugh punctuating his words. "I prefer to think of it as a mutually beneficial arrangement. I keep your secrets, and you… well, you ensure I'm properly compensated for the service."

He moved to his desk chair and sank into it, the leather creaking beneath his weight. How had it come to this? He'd thought he was finally free when Waldo Sr. had died two years ago. The old man had been bleeding him dry for decades, using what he knew about the adoption to extract regular "consulting fees." Payments that had strained his finances, but had been necessary to keep his secrets safe. And now here was the son, picking up right where his father had left off. But apparently, Waldo Sr. had made sure to pass along the profitable family secret to his son.

"Are you still there?" Waldo's voice cut through his thoughts.

"Yeah, I'm here." His voice was tight, controlled. "I'll bring your money," he spat the word, venom dripping from each syllable, "tonight."

"That's great!" The excitement in Waldo's voice was unrestrained. The sound of it made his skin crawl. "Shall we say nine o'clock? At my office?"

"Fine." The word was clipped, final.

"Perfect. Looking forward to it."

The call ended, and he sat in silence, staring at the darkened screen of his phone. Waldo's greed was predictable, almost comforting in its familiarity. But the revelation about Olivia and Tyson's visit to his office, that was a real problem.

He swept the cell phone on his desk to the floor in a sudden burst of rage. It clattered against the hardwood. He bent forward, elbows on knees, head in hands, and forced himself to think. The situation was spiraling out of control. Sooner or later, one of them would unravel everything and the truth would come out. About the adoption, what happened after, all of it. And then what?

Prison, most likely. Disgrace, certainly.

He straightened slowly, a calm settling over him as clarity emerged from the chaos of his thoughts. The solution was obvious, had been from the beginning. He'd just been reluctant to acknowledge it.

He moved to the small safe hidden behind a landscape painting on the eastern wall. The combination came automatically, his mother's birthday, a date etched into his memory. Inside, among various documents and a small stack of emergency cash, lay a 9 mm handgun. He withdrew it, feeling the weight of it in his palm. It had been years since he'd held it, longer still since he'd fired it, but the feel of it was familiar, almost comforting.

There was no other way. Waldo would never stop demanding money. Olivia would never stop digging into the past. Even Tyson might eventually stumble onto something he couldn't ignore.

The risks were too great. The potential costs too high.

The loose ends had to be tied up. Permanently.

Chapter Thirteen

The bell above the diner door jingled as Tyson held it open for Olivia, catching a whiff of her perfume as she passed. Then the familiar scents of frying meat and fresh coffee enveloped him, a comforting constant in Galesburg since his childhood. He noted how conversations dimmed momentarily as heads turned toward the entrance. Specifically, toward Olivia. Small-town curiosity at its finest. He guided her toward an empty booth by the window, aware of at least a dozen pairs of eyes tracking their movement across the floor.

"Looks like we're the main attraction," he said as they slid into opposite sides of the vinyl booth.

Olivia settled into her seat, her gaze sweeping the diner. "I'm getting that impression."

Margie, who'd been waitressing since Tyson was tall enough to see over the counter, approached with two glasses of water and a knowing smile.

"Chief, nice to see you with company today." Her eyes flicked to Olivia with undisguised interest.

"This is Olivia Lowell," he said, not offering any more information that needed. He didn't want the town rumor mill spinning any faster than it already was. "Olivia, this is Margie. She makes the best apple pie in Galesburg."

"Not only this side." Margie winked at Olivia. "Don't believe a word he says. My pie is the best in all of the state, period."

Olivia's smile seemed genuine. "I'll have to try it."

"You two know what you want, or should I give you a minute?" Margie pulled her order pad from her apron pocket.

"I'll have the open-faced roast beef sandwich," Tyson said without looking at the menu.

Olivia glanced briefly at the laminated page. "The chicken salad sounds good. And iced tea, please."

"Make that two iced teas," he added.

As Margie walked away, Olivia leaned forward. "Is there anyone in this place you don't know?"

The corner of his mouth twitched upward. "Probably not. Occupational hazard of being both the police chief and a local boy."

"And the source of all those stares?" Olivia nodded subtly toward the other patrons, several of whom were still glancing their way while pretending not to.

"That's all you. You're new and interesting. We don't get a lot of that around here. Plus—" He stopped himself, realizing he'd been about to comment on her appearance.

"Plus what?" Her eyebrow arched in question.

"Plus, you're having lunch with the chief of police, which makes you doubly interesting." He reached for his water glass, hoping the deflection wasn't too obvious.

She studied him for a moment, her expression unreadable. "I'm curious about something."

"Ask away." He tried to keep his tone casual, her tone put him on alert.

"Why did you leave the Los Angeles Police Department to come back here?"

His eyebrows rose. He shouldn't be surprised she'd done her homework.

A flush of color rose in her cheeks, but she didn't look away. "Just an internet search. I like to know who I'm working with."

Their iced teas arrived, creating a momentary pause in the conversation. Tyson watched as Olivia added a packet of sugar to hers, stirring with precise movements. He cataloged details, the careful way she handled the utensils, the slight furrow between her brows as she concentrated.

"So, we're working together now," he said after taking a sip of his tea.

"For the time being." Her tone carried a hint of caution, as if reminding both of them of the temporary nature of their arrangement.

Margie delivered their food, and he welcomed the distraction. The aroma of warm gravy and fresh bread made his stomach growl appreciatively.

"To answer your question," he said as he cut into his sandwich, "I left because I got homesick. Sounds simple, maybe even a little pathetic, but it's the truth."

"Los Angeles wasn't what you expected?"

"It was exactly what I expected. Busy, impersonal, full of cases that never got the attention they deserved because there were always a hundred more waiting." He paused, trying to articulate something he rarely discussed. "I was good at my job there, but I never felt…connected. Here, I know the people I'm protecting."

She nodded slowly, considering his words as she took a bite of her salad. "Why not Boston? Your sister lives there, right?"

"Boston's fine for visits. Kara and I get along great, but…" He searched for the right words. "Living in Los Angeles taught me I'm not a city boy. Boston's just another big city with worse weather."

Olivia looked out the window at the quiet main street, a thoughtful expression crossing her face. "I can see the appeal of knowing your neighbors. In DC, I've lived in the same building for three years and couldn't tell you the names of half the people on my floor."

Something in her voice, a note of wistfulness, caught his attention. He wondered if she was merely being polite or if Galesburg had resonated with her. The thought stirred a curiosity that veered into dangerous territory he wasn't sure he should explore.

He took another bite of his sandwich.

"Chief! How's that sandwich treating you?" called Ed Miller from two booths over, breaking into Tyson's thoughts.

"Can't complain, Ed," he answered with an easy smile, noting Olivia's careful observation of the exchange.

She took a sip of her tea. "This must be what it's like to dine with a celebrity."

"Hardly." He rolled his eyes, though her teasing tone lightened his chest.

Olivia laughed, a genuine sound that caught him off guard with its warmth. For a moment, the case that had brought them together receded into the background, and he found himself simply enjoying the company of the woman across the table.

"So, what exactly does your graphic design business involve?" he asked, genuinely curious. He'd noticed how she'd perked up whenever she mentioned her work. He wanted to see more of that side of her. The Olivia Lowell who existed beyond the secrets that had brought her to Galesburg.

Olivia set down her fork, and her expression shifted. Her eyes brightened, and her shoulders relaxed. "I do mostly branding work for small to mid-sized businesses," she said. "Logo design, marketing materials, website aesthetics. I help companies tell their visual story." Her hands moved as she spoke, elegant fingers sketching invisible designs in the air.

"There's something magical about distilling a business's entire identity into a mark that can be recognized in seconds."

The cautious, guarded woman who'd arrived in town had momentarily vanished, replaced by someone whose passion radiated from every gesture.

"How did you get started?" he asked, ignoring his half-eaten sandwich.

"I was always the nerdy kid with colored pencils and sketchbooks." She smiled, a genuine expression that reached her eyes. "In high school, I started designing flyers for school events. Then in college, I worked on a logo for a friend's start-up. After graduation, I took a corporate design job, but it was..."

"Constraining?" he offered when she paused.

"Exactly." She looked at him with a flash of appreciation for the understanding. "A few years ago, I quit and started my own business. Best decision I ever made, even with all the uncertainty."

He watched the subtle changes in her face as she spoke. The slight lift at the corner of her mouth when she mentioned quitting her job, the confident set of her jaw when referring to her business. He found it difficult to look away.

"Do you enjoy living in DC?" he asked, taking a sip of his tea.

Olivia's gaze drifted to the window, to the quiet main street of Galesburg with its familiar storefronts and unhurried pedestrians. "It's all I've ever known, really. The pace, the noise, the anonymity..." She turned back to him. "But lately I've been thinking I might be ready for a change."

The statement sent an unexpected current through his chest. He immediately tried to tamp down the reaction, reminding himself of the professional boundaries he needed to maintain. And yet, he couldn't help the thought that flashed unbidden across his mind. Could she be happy here?

The notion was ridiculous. She had a successful business in DC, a whole life he knew nothing about. Still, he said, "This place grows on you. Is there anyone back in DC who'd be sad to see you go?" The question came out before he could reconsider it. "I mean, if you ever did decide to make a change."

As soon as the words left his mouth, he knew how transparent the inquiry was. Olivia's knowing smile confirmed she'd caught his meaning precisely. The heat of embarrassment crept up his neck.

"No," she answered, her eyes holding his. "I have friends, of course, but I've always been somewhat of a loner. I spent most of my time with my mother." A shadow crossed her features at the mention of her mother, reminding him of the painful reason for her presence in Galesburg.

He absorbed this new information with more satisfaction than he had any right to feel. Single. The word echoed pleasantly in his mind.

"What about you?" Olivia asked, turning the tables with a slight curve to her lips. "Is there someone special in your life? Or does crime-fighting leave no time for romance?"

The teasing lilt in her voice made his pulse quicken. "No," he replied, matching her directness. "Since I've moved back to town, I've been too busy with the department." He traced the condensation on his glass with one finger, then added, "But Stephanie and Amelia have been on me to find a better work-life balance. They can't wait for me to settle down."

Olivia studied him over the rim of her glass. "Is that what you want? To settle down?"

He looked directly into her eyes, aware that his answer carried more weight than simple conversation warranted. The diner around them seemed to recede—the clink of silverware, murmured conversations, the sizzle from the grill—fading to background.

"If I find the right woman, yes," he said, his gaze never leaving hers. "I very much want that."

The moment stretched between them. He timed the slight rise and fall of Olivia's chest as she breathed. For a brief instant, he allowed himself to imagine a future where she was more than just a temporary visitor to Galesburg.

Then her phone buzzed on the table, shattering the connection. She glanced down, reaching for the device with casual familiarity. The openness in her expression vanished, replaced by a bloodless pallor that set alarm bells ringing in his head. Her fingers tightened around the phone, her knuckles whitening.

"What is it?" He leaned forward, his professional instincts on alert. "Olivia?"

She didn't answer immediately, her eyes fixed on the screen. When she looked up, the vulnerability in her expression pinched his heart.

"Someone…" She cleared her throat. "Someone sent me this." She turned the phone toward him.

The message glowed starkly against the dark screen. Stop digging or you'll join your mother.

Cold dread spread through his chest, a familiar sensation he'd experienced at crime scenes and in moments of genuine danger. But this time was different. The threat against Olivia triggered a protectiveness that momentarily clouded his vision.

He took the phone from her, noting the Unknown Number displayed at the top of the screen. His mind was already cataloging details. The timestamp. The exact wording. But beneath the professional assessment ran a current of raw emotion. Fury that someone would threaten Olivia, fear for her safety and an overwhelming need to protect her

"We need to go," he said, his voice pitched low. He signaled to Margie for the check. "I'll taking you back to the lake house."

Olivia nodded, her composure visibly reassembling itself though her face remained pale. She reached for her purse with steady hands that betrayed only the slightest tremor.

"Do you think it's connected to what happened to my mother?" she asked, voicing the question he'd been grappling with.

Margie approached with their bill.

"Everything's connected until proven otherwise," he replied. He handed Margie enough cash to cover their meal and a generous tip. "We'll talk in the car."

The walk to his SUV passed in tense silence. He scanned the street, the parked cars, the storefronts, looking for anything out of place, anyone paying too much attention. Small towns had their advantages when it came to security; strangers stood out, but they also bred complacency. He'd believed Galesburg was safe. Recent events were challenging that belief.

Once they were both inside the SUV, he pulled out his phone and dialed the station before even starting the engine.

"Revis," a voice answered after two rings.

"It's Tyson," he said. "I need you to trace a number that just sent a text to Olivia Lowell's phone. I'm sending you the details now." He forwarded the information from Olivia's phone.

"Threatening message?" Revis asked, his tone shifting to alert professionalism.

"Get everything you can on the sender. Location data if possible. Make it a priority."

"On it, Chief. I'll let you know as soon as I have anything."

He ended the call and pulled away from the curb. Beside him, Olivia remained silent, her earlier animation completely gone.

"You okay?" he asked.

"I'm fine." Her voice was steady, but her hands were clasped tightly in her lap. "It's not the first threat I've received since coming to Galesburg."

They drove in silence until he turned into the driveway of the rental house. He parked and looked at Olivia. "I need to check the house before you go in. It's standard procedure when there's been a threat."

She relented with a nod, waiting in the SUV as he approached the house. He drew his weapon, keeping it low against his leg as he circled the perimeter, checking windows and doors for signs of forced entry before heading inside. Finding nothing disturbed inside or out, he returned to the vehicle and signaled for Olivia to join him. She approached the house with cautious steps, her eyes scanning the property as if seeing it through new, more suspicious eyes.

Chapter Fourteen

Midnight ticked by but sleep continued to elude Olivia. She rolled onto her left side, then her right, bunching the pillow beneath her head. But the words from the threatening text message wouldn't stop scrolling through her mind on endless repeat. The sheets tangled around her legs as she shifted position yet again, sighing into the darkness.

Giving up on sleep for the moment, she kicked free of the twisted bedding and swung her feet to the floor. The cool hardwood beneath her toes provided a momentary anchor to reality as she reached for her robe, at the foot of the bed. She slipped her arms into the soft cotton sleeves and cinched the belt at her waist. The digital clock's red numbers glared at her: 12:27 a.m.

The hallway stretched before her, bathed in shadows broken only by the faint silver moonlight filtering through a window at the far end. She made her way down the stairs, one hand trailing along the banister, each creak of the old steps amplified in the quiet. The unfamiliar sounds of this house were so different from her apartment back in DC. Could she ever see herself living in a little town like Galesburg? Maybe even Galesburg? Her conversation with Tyson floated through her mind. It would be nice to have Stephanie nearby, to get to know her cousin. And Tyson. He wouldn't be why she'd stay in Galesburg, she thought. But he could be an added bonus, her subconscious shot back.

In the kitchen, she flicked on the under-cabinet lights rather than the harsh overhead fixture. The gentle glow created pools of amber across the countertops, lending the space an intimate feel. She reached for the kettle, filling it at the sink before setting it on the stove. The mundane ritual of preparing tea grounded her, giving her hands something to do while her thoughts continued their relentless spin. The threats. The dead ends trying to find her father. Tyson.

She pulled a mug from the cabinet, a cheerful yellow one with a chip on the rim, and selected a tea bag from the canister on the counter. Chamomile. Maybe it would help quiet her mind enough to eventually sleep.

This trip to Galesburg had veered so far from what she'd imagined. She leaned against the counter, waiting for the water to boil, and closed her eyes. She'd come looking for family, for roots. Instead, she'd found more questions and a text message that made her skin crawl.

Stephanie had been wonderful, welcoming her with open arms. Offering the photo album and Annalise's other things. There was so much warmth in Stephanie's eyes when she looked at Olivia, like she'd found a treasure she hadn't known was missing. It made her chest expand with hope that Amelia might also look at her like that one day.

The kettle whistled. Olivia moved it off the burner and poured the steaming water over the tea bag. And what of her birth father?

There had to be a reason that he had gone to such lengths to keep his identity hidden. More than just that he was married when she was conceived. She carried the mug between her palms, the heat seeping into her skin as she moved toward the living room.

What if he was truly dangerous? The text message pulsed in her memory: Stop digging or you'll join your mother.

Her fingers tightened around the mug. The tea sloshed dangerously close to the rim as she settled onto the sofa, tucking her feet beneath her.

And then there was Tyson.

Her stomach fluttered at the mere thought of him, an involuntary reaction that annoyed her almost as much as the man himself sometimes did. Chief Tyson Morrow with his stern jaw, and watchful eyes that softened unexpectedly at times, revealing glimpses of something gentle beneath the professional exterior.

The tea warmed her from the inside as she took a cautious sip then set the mug aside. She couldn't remember ever meeting a man who frustrated her as thoroughly as Tyson did. Or one who attracted her so powerfully. The memory of his brief touches, the electricity that seemed to arc between them whenever he stood too close. The way his gaze sometimes lingered on her mouth when she spoke. Stop it.

She pinched the bridge of her nose, forcing the thoughts away. She shouldn't feel attracted to him at all. She hadn't come to Galesburg for a romance, especially not with a man so deeply embedded in the community. She was there to learn about her past and to finally establish some roots now that her adoptive mother was gone.

To find family. To belong somewhere, to someone.

She took another sip, letting the warmth and the subtle sweetness of the honey she'd added settle her nerves. A movement outside caught her eye, sending a jolt of fear through her until she realized that it was just Tyson's SUV in the driveway. The sight of it, of him out there presumably to protect her, sent a heated, flutter cascading through her chest that had nothing to do with the tea.

She turned and padded back to the kitchen. She set her half-finished mug on the counter and reached for another from the cabinet. She poured hot water from the still-warm kettle over the tea bag, added a spoonful of honey and stirred before taking the mug to the front entryway, where she paused long enough to slip on canvas sneakers.

She picked up the mug again, balancing it carefully as she unlatched the front door. The night air rushed to meet her, cooler than she'd expected, carrying the sweet perfume of nearby jasmine and the earthy scent of recent rain. The almost full moon illuminated the steps and walkway in a soft silver glow.

Tyson spotted her immediately. His car door opened, and he unfolded himself from the driver's seat.

"I thought you might like some tea to warm you up," she said, extending the mug as she drew closer.

His fingers brushed hers as he accepted it, the brief contact sending a shock of awareness along her skin. "Thank you, although I think the tea may work against me." The corner of his mouth quirked up. "I'm supposed to be staying alert."

She cocked her head, studying him. The moonlight carved shadows beneath his cheekbones, highlighting the strong line of his jaw. "Were you planning to sit out here all night?"

The sheepish look on his face made him appear boyish. "Maybe not all night."

She smiled shyly at him, wrapping her arms around herself against the night chill. "Well, at least sit on the porch. It'll be more comfortable."

He hesitated briefly before nodding. As they walked back up the path to the house, she was acutely aware of his presence beside her.

The porch swing creaked as they settled onto it, the chains swaying gently as they found their balance. She tucked one leg beneath her, angling herself toward him. The silhouettes of the nearby trees formed a protective barrier around the property. Fireflies flickered around the shrubs, their white lights blinking like tiny stars.

They sipped their tea in companionable silence for a moment, the swing moving in a gentle arc beneath them, the rhythmic motion almost hypnotic.

"My mother loved nights like this," Tyson said, his voice low and rich in the darkness.

She glanced at him, catching the softness that had entered his expression. "We don't have many nights like this in the city. I think part of my problem getting to sleep is how quiet it is here. No ambulance sirens or car horns honking." She nudged his arm playfully with her elbow. "It's unnatural."

He laughed, the sound deep and genuine. "Yeah, it took me a while to get used to the ambient noise when I lived in Los Angeles and then again to the quiet when I moved back here." He gazed out at the yard, at the dancing fireflies and swaying tree branches. "But I vastly prefer this. Being in Galesburg makes me feel closer to my mother."

The wistful note in his voice touched her. "I don't know if I was ever really close to my mother," she said quietly. "My adoptive mother, I mean."

She added, "I knew she loved me. I was never neglected or anything like that. But she was always busy. She was very career-oriented, and sometimes it seemed like I was an afterthought."

The swing creaked beneath them as Tyson shifted, his thigh now pressing lightly against hers. He didn't respond immediately, just watched her with those intent eyes that seemed to see more than she wanted to reveal.

"She worked a lot," she continued, the words spilling out now that she'd started. "Important dinners, late meetings, business trips. There were a lot of nannies and housekeepers when I was little. She always made sure I had everything I needed, but…" She trailed off, surprised by how raw the old wound still was.

She held her breath for a moment, a tightness constricting her chest as she waited for his reaction. She'd never admitted those feelings about her mother to anyone before. The vulnerability left her feeling exposed. But he simply looked at her, his eyes steady and understanding, no judgment shadowing his features.

An owl hooted, its call echoing through the trees, and the night wrapped around them creating a small, private world on the porch swing.

"I asked her once why she'd decided to adopt," she continued, her voice quiet but steadier now. The words flowed more easily with that first barrier broken. "She said, 'I wanted someone to love me.'"

She fell silent, watching the dance of fireflies among the bushes. The simple statement had shaped her understanding of her place in her mother's life. A solution to her mother's loneliness.

"I guess I can't really fault her for that." A humorless laugh escaped her. "I'm here in Galesburg for the same reason. Looking for a connection with someone so that I don't feel so alone in the world." The parallel hadn't fully struck her until this moment. "But I always thought maybe any child would have done."

His warm hand covered hers where it rested on the swing between them. The unexpected contact sent a current of awareness up her arm.

"I think we're all looking for a connection," he said, his voice low and resonant in the quiet night. "No one wants to be alone in the world."

The simple truth of his words settled into her, creating a bridge over the distance they'd maintained.

She turned her hand beneath his, their palms meeting, fingers intertwining. His skin was warm against hers, rough with calluses. She looked up and found him watching her, his eyes dark and intent. The air between them seemed to charge with electricity, making it suddenly difficult to draw a full breath.

Neither moved for a heartbeat. She wasn't sure who leaned in first, but then his lips were touching hers gently, almost tentatively, a question more than a demand.

The softness of that first contact undid her. Her free hand moved to his shoulder, feeling the solid warmth of him beneath the fabric of his shirt. His scent enveloped her, woody and distinctly him. The kiss deepened as his hand came up to cradle her cheek.

The kiss that began as a gentle exploration quickly transformed into something more urgent. The sweet tenderness gave way to heat as his arm circled her waist, drawing her closer. Her fingers threaded through his hair, short and surprisingly soft against her skin. She tasted tea and honey on his lips. The firm pressure of his mouth against hers, the strength in the arms that held her, the slight creak of the swing as they shifted closer. Her breath came in short gasps when they briefly separated before coming together again with increased urgency.

A sharp electronic chime cut through the moment like a knife. She pulled back, disoriented by the intrusion. His chest rose and fell rapidly, his eyes dark with desire. The look sent a fresh wave of heat spiraling through her.

She considered ignoring it. The desire to drag him upstairs to her bedroom was overwhelming, a visceral need to continue what they'd started, to feel his skin against hers without barriers.

With a reluctant sigh, she pulled the device from her pocket and squinted at the notification. "It's an email from the DNA lab."

Her heart rate picked up again for an entirely different reason. With trembling fingers, she opened the message and scanned the contents.

The technical language was a blur, but she found the lines that mattered easily.

DNA analysis confirms a first cousin relationship between Olivia Lowell and Stephanie Santini with 99.9% certainty.

Olivia looked up from the screen, the joy bubbling up inside her was almost too big to contain.

"It's the DNA results," she said, her voice catching. "Stephanie and I are cousins. Annalise is my biological mother."

The words hung in the night air, solid and real in a way they hadn't been before. Not just hope or possibility, but fact. Scientific proof of her connection to these people, this place.

She belonged here.

The realization hit with unexpected force, bringing tears to her eyes.

Tyson's expression softened as the emotions played across her face. "That's wonderful, Olivia," he said, squeezing her hand gently. "I know how much this means to you."

The confirmation of her biological connection to Annalise sat alongside the lingering warmth of his kiss. One anchored her to the past. The other offering a potential future she hadn't anticipated finding in Galesburg.

THE TOASTER POPPED with a cheerful ding, startling Olivia from her thoughts. Morning light streamed through the kitchen windows, casting golden rectangles across the counter where she stood in her robe, hair still tousled from sleep. She'd been awake since five, her mind too full for proper rest, and had finally given up at six, padding downstairs to make breakfast. Steam rose from her mug of freshly brewed tea, curling into the air as she reached for the toast and placed it on her waiting plate.

The quiet morning routine should have been soothing, but her thoughts kept circling back to the night before. To Tyson.

After she'd received the DNA results, a strange shift occurred. Tyson had been genuinely happy for her, she'd seen it in the crinkles at the corners of his eyes, the warmth of his smile. But something had changed in the atmosphere between them, as if the confirmation of her relation to Stephanie and Amelia had made their connection more complicated rather than simpler.

"It's getting late," he'd said, untangling himself from their half-embrace on the porch swing. "You should get some rest."

She scraped butter across her toast, watching it melt into the warm bread. He'd seen her into the house and made sure she locked the door before he drove away, the red taillights of his SUV disappearing down the long driveway.

The butter knife clattered against the plate as she set it down. She lifted her mug, inhaling the fragrant steam before taking a careful sip. The tea was still too hot, searing a path down her throat, but the mild pain was a welcome distraction from the memory of Tyson's lips on hers.

That kiss. God, that kiss.

She closed her eyes, and the sensation washed over her again. How his lips had parted hers, gentle at first and then with increasing urgency. The way her body had responded instantly, a liquid warmth pooling low in her belly, every nerve ending suddenly alive.

She'd never felt such an attraction to a man before. It wasn't just physical, though heaven knew that element was powerful enough. There was something about the way he listened when she spoke, really listened, the quiet strength he projected without dominating. And the tenderness that occasionally broke through his professional demeanor.

She carried her breakfast to the kitchen table by the window, sinking into a chair with a sigh. Outside, early morning mist clung to the surface of the lake.

She would be going back to DC eventually. Her life was there—her job, her apartment, her few friends. Galesburg was just a place to find answers about her past, not to build a future. Starting a relationship with Tyson would be impractical at best, potentially painful at worst. Long-distance relationships rarely worked, and she wasn't planning to relocate permanently to a small town, no matter how charming it might be or how strong her biological connections to the place.

The tea cooled in her mug as she stared out at the misty landscape. A different thought slipped into her mind. Did something have to come of it?

Plenty of people just had flings. Brief, passionate encounters with no expectations beyond mutual pleasure. No commitments, no messy emotions, just two consenting adults enjoying each other's company for a limited time.

The concept made her feel strangely off-kilter, as if she'd stepped onto ground that shifted beneath her feet. She'd never had a fling or a one-night stand. Her relationships had been few and carefully considered, usually developing from friendship into something more. The idea of pursuing Tyson purely for physical satisfaction, knowing from the outset that it would end when she left town…

A voice inside her head whispered, *There's no time like the present.*

She shook her head sharply, dismissing the thought. That wasn't who she was. She couldn't separate physical intimacy from emotional connection so neatly, and pretending otherwise would only lead to hurt feelings. Most likely her own.

Her toast sat half eaten on her plate, the tea in her mug gone tepid. With a sigh, she pushed away from the table. She needed to shower and dress, to focus on the day ahead. The DNA confirmation opened new doors for her investigation into her past. She should be concentrating on that, not mooning over the police chief like a teenager with her first crush.

She carried her dishes to the sink, rinsing them before setting them in the dishwasher. The simple domestic task helped center her, pushing thoughts of Tyson to the periphery of her mind.

As she climbed the stairs to her bedroom, she resolved to maintain a polite distance from him going forward. The kiss had been wonderful, but pursuing anything further would only complicate her already complex situation in Galesburg.

An hour later, showered and dressed, she drove toward Amelia's Café. The DNA results burned like a happy secret in her purse, concrete proof of what she'd suspected since arriving in Galesburg. She couldn't wait to see Stephanie's face when she shared the news that they were definitely family.

The bell above the door jingled cheerfully as she entered the café. Relief washed over her when she saw only Stephanie and another young woman behind the counter, no sign of Amelia, whose cold reception had been a persistent shadow over her search. Stephanie looked up from the coffee machine she was wiping down, her eyes immediately lighting up.

"Olivia!" Stephanie's smile spread wide across her face. "It's so good to see you."

She approached the counter, unable to contain her own smile. "I have news," she said, keeping her voice low despite the empty café.

Stephanie's eyebrows shot up. "About the DNA tests?" She leaned forward eagerly, elbows on the counter.

She nodded, feeling a rush of warmth as Stephanie's excitement mirrored her own. Her cousin squealed.

"Do you have a minute to talk?" she asked.

"Just give me a minute," Stephanie promised, her eyes dancing with anticipation. "Go grab a table. What can I get you?"

"A breakfast tea would be great," she replied, moving toward a corner table that offered a bit of privacy.

The smell of coffee and cinnamon rolls wrapped around the interior of the café. She set her phone on the table, the DNA results queued up and ready to share. Stephanie approached with a steaming mug of tea. She set the mug down and slid into the chair opposite Olivia.

"You should have told me you prefer tea," Stephanie said.

She smiled, wrapping her fingers around the warm mug. "There's a lot we need to learn about each other, cousin." She held out her phone so Stephanie could see the screen, watching her face carefully.

Stephanie took the phone with reverent fingers. "For real? We're cousins?" Her voice trembled as her eyes scanned the results.

She couldn't hold back her grin. "They say DNA doesn't lie. According to the lab, we are cousins, maternally related." Saying it aloud made it more real.

Stephanie squealed again, louder this time, and set the phone on the table to reach across and pull Olivia into a hug. The embrace was awkward, but Olivia laughed and leaned into it, feeling her heart lighten at Stephanie's unconditional acceptance. This was what family should feel like.

"I can't believe it," Stephanie said as she settled back

into her seat, eyes shining. "I believed you, but seeing it on paper…"

"I know exactly what you mean," Olivia replied.

Stephanie picked up the phone again, staring at the results. "Can you send me this? I want to show it to Mom." She looked up, expression hopeful. "Maybe having DNA proof of who you are will get her to open up more."

Some of her joy dissipated at the mention of Amelia. "Yes, of course," she said. She took back her phone and forwarded the results to Stephanie's number.

Stephanie looked at her thoughtfully, seeming to sense the shift in her mood. "Mom will come around," she said, reaching across to touch her hand briefly. "She's stubborn, but she's not unreasonable."

Stephanie cleared her throat and leaned forward, a sly expression replacing her earlier earnestness. "So," she began, "I heard that you and Tyson were spotted around town together quite a bit yesterday."

The abrupt change of subject caught her off guard. Her mind instantly flashed to Tyson beside her on the porch swing the night before, the weight of his arm around her shoulders, the way he'd pulled her closer until their lips met.

She blinked, suddenly aware that Stephanie was watching her with knowing eyes. She could feel a blush creeping up her neck, betraying her thoughts more effectively than any words could have.

Stephanie gave her a sly look and grinned. "Aha."

She shifted in her seat. "Aha, nothing. He was helping me track down people who might know the name of my birth father."

Stephanie didn't look convinced, but she leaned closer, her expression turning more serious. "Did you have any luck?"

"No," she said, the word heavy on her tongue. "From the

yearbook in the stuff you gave me, I found Annalise's best friend, Sarah. She's a therapist in town." She took a sip of tea, letting the warmth slide down her throat, wishing it could wash away the disappointment as easily.

Stephanie's eyebrows shot up in surprise. "Sarah Garrett?" she asked.

"Yes," she said, nodding. "Do you know her?"

"Only a little. Mostly in passing." Stephanie frowned, her brow furrowing. "Mom has never once mentioned Sarah and Aunt Annalise being friends. Not once."

Olivia fought to keep her expression neutral. Amelia seemed to have omitted a lot of potentially useful information.

"Well," she continued, "Sarah says she doesn't know who my biological father was. She says Annalise never told her." Stephanie must have caught the disbelief in her tone because she tilted her head questioningly. She sighed and elaborated. "I just… I got the sense she knew more than she was saying. But I couldn't press her."

"Because Tyson was there?" Stephanie guessed.

"Partly," she admitted. "But also because she's a therapist. She knows how to deflect questions and keep secrets." She ran her fingers through her hair, a habit when frustration mounted. "But my adoption files were unsealed, and I learned the name of the attorney who facilitated the adoption. I thought that might lead somewhere."

Stephanie looked encouraged. "It sounds promising."

"I thought so too," Olivia replied. "But he couldn't help me either."

Stephanie covered her hand with hers. "I'm sorry you keep hitting dead ends," she said, her eyes sincere. Then the corners of her mouth quirked up. "But Tyson has been of help, right?" The sly tone was back, impossible to miss.

Olivia gave her cousin an exasperated look but couldn't

maintain it. A smile tugged at the corners of her mouth despite her best efforts.

"Tyson was very helpful," she conceded. Then she recalled how he hadn't let her press Sarah for an answer, even though she was sure Sarah knew more than she'd told them. Her smile faltered. "And a little frustrating."

Stephanie laughed loudly, the sound bright in the quiet café. "Yeah, that's Tyson. But you get used to it."

"I know he means well," she found herself saying.

"He's a good man," Stephanie agreed, her expression softening. "One of the best in Galesburg. It's nice to see him taking an interest in something besides work for once."

Heat crept back into Olivia's cheeks. "He's just doing his job," she insisted, though the memory of his hands on her hips suggested otherwise.

Stephanie's expression made it clear she didn't believe that for a second, but she didn't push. Instead, she took a sip of her coffee and changed the subject. "So, what's your next step? In looking for your father, I mean."

Her shoulders slumped. "I'm not sure," she admitted. "I've hit all the obvious leads. Sarah and the attorney were my best hope. Maybe Amelia will open up once she sees the DNA results." Though she didn't hold much hope for that possibility.

"Mom can be stubborn," Stephanie acknowledged. "But family means everything to her, even when she's being difficult about it." Stephanie squeezed her hand again. "And you're family. The tests prove it."

Family. The word was still new and precious to her. Now she had a cousin sitting across from her, sharing coffee and confidences. It wasn't the complete answer she'd been seeking, but it was more than she'd had before coming to Galesburg.

Chapter Fifteen

Tyson stared at Annalise's high school senior portrait. The colors had worn away with time, much like the case itself, faded but refusing to disappear completely. He traced the outline of the hit-and-run report with his index finger, willing the words to reveal something everyone had missed. But Olivia's face kept intruding, pushing aside the cold facts of the case with the warm memory of her lips against his.

The hit-and-run file lay open on his desk, the sparce pieces spread out like a puzzle he couldn't solve. Outside his glass-walled office, the bullpen hummed with the typical morning activity, phones ringing, keyboards clicking, officers comparing notes on ongoing cases.

None of it held his attention.

That kiss. That perfect kiss on Olivia's front porch.

The memory of it washed over him again. The soft pressure of her mouth. The faint scent of her perfume mingling with the night air. His heart had hammered against his ribs in anticipation. Best kiss of his life. No contest.

He rubbed his hand across his jaw, surprised to find himself smiling. He glanced around, irrationally concerned that someone might have read his thoughts. The bullpen continued its morning routine, oblivious to their chief's romantic distraction.

He tapped his pen rhythmically against the desk calendar.

Olivia wasn't just getting under his skin. She was burrowing straight to his core. The tension between them had been palpable from day one. It wasn't just attraction, not anymore.

He thought about how her eyes had softened last night as they sat on her porch swing, her guard lowering as she talked about her family. The vulnerability in her voice when she admitted how alone she was sometimes had touched him. He had wanted to tell her then that she was more than enough. That he saw her. But the words had caught in his throat.

He shifted in his chair, uncomfortable with how deeply she'd gotten to him in such a short time. In his years of police work, he'd learned to keep people at arm's length. Emotional distance was a survival tactic. With Olivia, though, every defensive wall he'd built seemed to crumble.

The thought surfaced before he could stop it. She was a woman he could fall in love with.

The realization jolted him like a physical shock. He sat up straighter, his hand freezing mid-tap against the calendar. Where the hell had that come from? They'd shared one kiss, one admittedly earth-shattering kiss, but love? That was premature. Reckless, even.

And yet. There was something about Olivia that called to him, something beyond her sharp intelligence, the way her smile transformed her entire face, or the vulnerability she'd trusted him enough to reveal. Each layer he discovered made him want to dig deeper, to know all of her.

A flash of movement caught his attention. He spotted Officer Revis weaving between desks, moving with unusual urgency.

His police instincts kicked in immediately, his body tensing in response to the young officer's apparent distress.

He stood, pushing thoughts of Olivia aside as Revis approached his door, his face flushed. Whatever had him running through the station wouldn't be good news.

Tyson pulled open his office door before Revis could knock. "What is it?"

The officer braced one hand against the doorframe, chest heaving. "Chief, it's bad." He took a quick breath. "We just got a call about a possible homicide."

The word landed between them with the weight of a concrete block. Homicide. In Galesburg, violent crime was rare. Murder was practically unheard-of.

"Where?"

"Emerson & Associates." Revis straightened his posture, regaining his composure. "The receptionist came in this morning to find her boss's office torn apart." He paused, swallowing hard. "Sir, Waldo Emerson is dead."

TYSON PUSHED PAST the officers at the entrance of Emerson & Associates, the familiar weight of dread settling in his stomach as he nodded to the uniformed officer stationed at the door and lifted the yellow crime scene tape without a word. The atmosphere inside the law office's reception area was stifling with the particular heaviness that only violent death could bring.

"Chief," Officer Mingnala said, nodding, "we've secured the perimeter. No signs of forced entry." The young officer flipped open his notebook. "Call came in at 8:17 a.m. from Catalina Danvers, Emerson's receptionist for the past eight years. She arrived to open the office and found the front door unlocked. When she went to check Emerson's office, she found him on the floor behind his desk. It looked like there'd been a struggle. Papers everywhere, furniture overturned."

"Any sign of robbery?"

"She didn't check. Said she saw the body and ran straight out to call 911." Officer Mingnala glanced up from his notes.

"Emerson's wallet was still on him, watch too, when we arrived. But his office was definitely searched."

The narrow hallway stretched before him, lined with framed law degrees and awards. The Emerson family legacy displayed in mahogany and glass. His footsteps echoed against the polished hardwood as he moved toward the office at the end of the hall, where a different kind of legacy now waited.

A camera flash illuminated the doorway momentarily. Tyson paused at the threshold, allowing his eyes to adjust to the tableau of violence within. Waldo Emerson lay sprawled on his back, arms splayed outward. Two dark circles marked his chest where the bullets had entered, the crisp white of his dress shirt now stained a rusty brown.

"Hell of a mess," Tyson muttered, though it wasn't just the body he referred to.

The office looked like it had been hit by a localized hurricane. Papers blanketed the floor in drifts of white and manila. Filing cabinets stood open, their contents disgorged across the expensive carpet. The two leather visitor's chairs had been overturned, and glass from a shattered picture frame glinted in the morning light streaming through partially closed blinds.

He crouched beside the body, careful to avoid the congealed blood that had pooled beneath Waldo. The lawyer's expensive watch had broken, probably when he'd fallen. It was stopped at 9:47 p.m., roughly twelve hours ago. Rigor mortis had set in fully, confirming the timeline. He leaned closer, noting the powder burns around the entry wounds.

"Two shots to the chest," Tyson said to no one in particular. "The killer wanted to make sure he died."

His gaze tracked to the blood spatter pattern on the bookcase behind where Waldo must have been standing when he was shot. The directional spray indicated he'd been facing his killer, backing up maybe. Not entirely unexpected, then.

The brass shell casings winked at him from near the door, 9 mm. The shooter hadn't bothered to collect them. So not a professional.

His mind drifted back to yesterday when he'd spoken to Waldo. He'd believed the lawyer when he'd said he didn't know anything about Olivia's adoption case. It looked like Waldo was a good actor because he didn't for a minute believe Waldo's untimely death coming so soon after his visit was just a coincidence.

A camera flash pulled him back to the present. The crime scene technician, Adams, photographed the shell casings before carefully placing them in an evidence bag.

"Make sure you get the blood spatter on the bookcase," Tyson instructed. "And check for prints on the doorknob and light switch."

He rose, his knees protesting the movement. He moved to Waldo's desk, which bore the brunt of the apparent search. Drawers had been pulled completely out, their contents dumped onto the floor. The computer remained untouched. Password protected, no doubt.

Beneath a scattered pile of legal briefs, a leather-bound notebook lay open. There was a string of numbers and letters on it. A case file number maybe. He slipped his phone from his pocket and took a surreptitious photo.

His gaze returned to Waldo's body. The man may have been keeping a dangerous secret, but he hadn't deserved this. No one did.

"What did you know?" Tyson whispered.

The office remained silent save for the methodical clicks of the camera and the quiet murmur of officers in the hallway. But he was certain of one thing. Waldo Emerson had died because he knew something about Olivia's adoption case. Somewhere in this chaos lay the connection he needed to prove that.

He turned to the two officers waiting by the door, their faces pinched with the particular unease that murder scenes always brought.

"Bag everything in the office that isn't a client file, notes or electronics," he instructed. "I'll work on getting a warrant for the files and the computers." But it wouldn't be easy. Even with Waldo's death he'd expect the other attorneys at the firm to try and stop the warrant.

He crouched again, this time beside the overturned trash bin. Several crumpled papers had spilled onto the carpet. He smoothed one out carefully. A lunch receipt from yesterday, after Tyson's visit. A second piece of paper was a torn sheet from a legal pad, blank except for a coffee ring stain. The third made his pulse quicken. Another legal pad sheet with a name and a date scrawled in Waldo's distinctive, slanted handwriting: Annalise Farr. 1995.

He held it up to the light. The pen had pressed hard, leaving deep indentations in the yellow paper. Waldo had written her name with urgency.

"Got anything?" Officer Mingnala asked, moving closer. The younger man started with the department before Tyson arrived, but he was sharp-eyed and methodical. Exactly what he needed on this case.

"Maybe." He slipped the paper into an evidence bag. "Waldo told me yesterday he didn't know anything about the adoption case I was investigating. But this—" he tapped the bag "—this suggests otherwise."

The crime scene technicians had finished photographing the main areas and were now collecting fibers from the carpet near the body.

He moved carefully through the debris on the floor, examining scattered papers and torn folders.

His attention shifted to the desk phone. He'd need a warrant for the official phone logs, but… He pressed a button on the base of the phone, and the digital screen illuminated, showing recent calls. He noted the outgoing call Waldo had made at 12:17 p.m. yesterday. Just twenty minutes after he and Olivia had left the law offices.

He considered the timeline. He'd spoken to Waldo in the late morning about Olivia's adoption case. Waldo had denied knowing anything, but that was apparently a lie. Waldo had most likely called his client from the adoption, maybe to warn him that he and Olivia were asking questions. Or maybe to leverage what he knew about the client and attempted blackmail. It would explain the ransacking. The client killed Waldo and then took whatever he could that might tie him to Olivia's adoption and Waldo's involvement. There was no sign of forced entry, so Waldo had to have let his killer in.

A chill crawled up Tyson's spine as a new thought surfaced. If the killer was systematically eliminating everyone connected to this adoption case, there was another potential target. Olivia, the child who had been adopted thirty years ago and whose very existence revealed his secret.

A sense of urgency gripped him. He turned to the evidence technician closest to him. "I need to put a rush on processing this evidence. This case takes precedence over anything else the lab is working on." The tech nodded and Tyson turned to Officer Mingnala. "Let's get going on procuring the phone records for Waldo's office, cell and home lines. I want to know everyone he spoke to in the last twenty-four hours."

Fear pressed down on him as he stepped back into the hallway. Two people were already dead. He wouldn't allow Olivia to become the third.

Chapter Sixteen

Olivia burst through the glass doors of the Galesburg police station, her heart hammering in her chest. The reception area smelled like industrial cleaner and stale coffee. She approached the desk where a female officer sat, her dark hair pulled back in a severe bun. The woman's expression was neutral, professional, a blank canvas that revealed nothing about the rumors tearing through Galesburg.

"I need to see Chief Morrow," she said.

Before the officer could respond, a familiar figure emerged from the hallway behind the desk. Tyson's face was etched with the kind of weariness that confirmed her worst fears before he even spoke.

"Olivia." His voice was low, a rough texture to it that hadn't been there yesterday. "Come back to my office."

She followed him through the bullpen, the tension visible in his shoulders. Other officers glanced up as they passed, their curious eyes lingering on her just a second too long.

Tyson's office was a rectangle of controlled chaos. Files stacked at precise angles, a whiteboard covered in his angular handwriting, a jacket hung carefully on a hook by the door. She was barely across the threshold when the words tumbled out of her.

"Tyson, it's going around town that Waldo Emerson was murdered. Is it true?" The question hung between them.

He waved her to a chair, not meeting her eyes as he leaned against his desk, half sitting on its edge. "Unfortunately, it is."

The confirmation struck her like a physical blow. She sank into the chair. The room tilted, the edges of her vision blurring before snapping back into sharp focus. "How?" The word escaped as barely more than a breath.

He crossed his arms over his chest. "He was shot. Twice."

"This is..." She searched for words that could contain the horror. "Unbelievable. Yesterday we were asking him about my birth father. And today he's dead."

His jaw tightened. "I can't dismiss the connection. Especially not after the threats that have been made against you. It's too much of a coincidence that Emerson was killed immediately after we saw him."

He pushed himself off the desk and began to pace, three steps one way, three steps back, trapped in the confines of the office. "I'm looking into who he spoke with after we left his office but..."

He stopped pacing abruptly. He crouched before her chair, putting himself at eye level. He took her hands in his. A jolt of electricity went through her at the contact.

"I'd like to assign you protection," he said, his voice gentle but firm.

Her heart fluttered wildly, partly from his proximity and partly from the fear his words confirmed. If he thought she needed protection, then the danger was real. Not just paranoia or coincidence.

She allowed herself a moment to feel the weight of his hands around hers, to draw strength from the contact. "I don't think that's necessary," she said.

His thumb traced small, unconscious circles on the backs of her hands. "You've already been threatened," he said, "and this person is dangerous."

His eyes searched hers. “Maybe…” She watched the internal debate play out on his face, the tightening around his eyes, the slight downturn of his mouth. “I really think you’d be safer back in DC.”

She smiled sadly, aware of how close their faces were. “If Waldo’s killer wants me dead, he’ll find me in DC. At least here…”

The words caught in her throat. At least here she had him to protect her. The thought materialized with startling clarity, but she swallowed it back. It was too presumptuous, too revealing of feelings she barely understood herself. And yet, sitting here with Tyson’s hands wrapped around hers, his concerned eyes fixed on her face, she couldn’t deny the truth of it.

Silence. She suddenly felt vulnerable, as if she’d revealed too much by what she hadn’t said. She straightened her back and gently pulled her hands from his. The loss of contact left her fingertips strangely cold.

“I understand what you’re saying, and I appreciate your concern,” Olivia said. She folded her newly freed hands in her lap, knuckles pressing together until they whitened. Inside, her thoughts churned, the murder, the threats, this unexpected attraction to Tyson, all of it swirling together into something dark and overwhelming.

She forced herself to breathe, to think through the fog of fear and confusion. Retreating to DC wouldn’t solve anything. It might even make things worse, isolating her from the very place where answers lay buried. Besides, she rebelled against the idea of running away.

She attempted to lighten the mood. “I’m not sure Stephanie would appreciate your advice though,” she said, a small, strained smile tugging at her lips. “She was just encouraging me to extend my stay in Galesburg.”

•

Tyson stood and walked around his desk to sit in his chair. She wished she knew what he was thinking.

"I think we should speak to Sarah again," she said, leaning forward in her chair. "Maybe with all that's happened she'll open up about whatever it is she's keeping from us."

Tyson tapped his temple with his index finger, a gesture she'd noticed several times during their conversations. She suppressed a smile at the now-familiar habit. It was something she could predict about him, a tiny window into his thought process.

Tyson's hand dropped back to his desk. "That's a good idea." He looked across the desk at her, his gaze direct and unguarded. The intensity in his eyes sent heat flooding through her, starting somewhere in her chest and radiating outward until even her cheeks were warm. "And if I can't convince you to go somewhere safe," he said, his voice dropping, taking on a rough edge that scraped against her nerves like sandpaper, "I guess I'll have to keep you by my side."

A shiver of attraction ran through her at his words, so potent she had to press her palms flat against her thighs to ground herself. There was professional concern in his statement, of course, but underneath that was emotion that made her breath catch and her heart accelerate.

The moment stretched between them, charged with possibilities neither of them was ready to name. Outside Tyson's office, the station continued its business. But sitting across from him, she knew that whatever came next, she wouldn't be facing it alone.

OLIVIA STOOD BESIDE Tyson in the therapy center's parking lot, the afternoon sun beating down on her shoulders as they watched Sarah climb out of her sedan. A knot of anticipation tightened in her stomach. Sarah hadn't noticed them yet, her attention focused on gathering her belongings from the passenger seat, and Olivia used those precious seconds to study her. This woman held pieces of her past, fragments of her origin story that she'd kept locked away for three decades.

When Sarah finally turned and spotted them, her body went rigid. Her eyes widened, then narrowed, a flash of panic quickly masked by professional composure. The leather purse she'd been adjusting on her shoulder slipped before she hitched it back up with a quick, defensive motion. Sarah began walking toward the building entrance, her pace noticeably brisk.

"Sarah," Tyson called out, his voice carrying quiet authority. Not intimidating, but impossible to ignore.

Sarah didn't slow down. If anything, her steps quickened as she called back over her shoulder. "I'm sorry, Chief. I'm late for an appointment." Her voice was clipped and dismissive.

She and Tyson matched Sarah's pace, the three of them performing an awkward dance across the parking lot. Olivia caught the scent of Sarah's perfume, a scent that was expensive and clean. The woman's hair was pulled back in a perfect knot at the nape of her neck, not a strand out of place.

"This will only take a moment, Sarah," Tyson said, "and it's important."

Sarah paused at the door of the building's entrance. Her hand rested on the handle, but she didn't pull it open. Instead, she turned to face them, her expression carefully composed. Her eyes darted from Tyson to Olivia then back to Tyson.

"I've told you," Sarah said, addressing Tyson while pointedly avoiding further eye contact with Olivia. "I don't know anything that can help you."

The dismissal in her tone sparked a flash of anger in Olivia. "I think we all know that is not true."

Sarah's head swung toward her, eyes wide with surprise

at the direct challenge. Her lips parted, ready to deliver what Olivia was certain would be another denial.

Tyson stepped forward before Sarah could speak, his movement subtle but effective in reclaiming control of the conversation.

"Sarah," he said, his voice now heavy with significance, "Waldo Emerson was found dead, murdered, earlier today."

Olivia watched Sarah's face intently, cataloging every minute reaction. She knew Tyson was doing the same; it was why he'd delivered the news so abruptly, hoping to catch an unguarded response.

Sarah froze. The color drained from her face.

Tyson took a step closer to Sarah. Olivia noticed how he dropped his shoulders, making himself appear less imposing. His voice lowered to barely above a whisper, ensuring no passersby could overhear.

"Sarah, if you know anything, now is the time to tell me."

Olivia held her breath, watching as Sarah's professional facade crumbled. The therapist swallowed hard, her eyelids fluttering rapidly. She recognized the calculations happening behind them, weighing options, considering consequences, determining how much to reveal.

After what felt like an eternity, Sarah gave a small, almost imperceptible nod, the movement so slight that Olivia might have missed it if she hadn't been studying the woman so intently.

The fear in Sarah's eyes was unmistakable now. Whatever she knew, whatever connection existed between her, Annalise and Waldo Emerson, it frightened her.

"Not here," Sarah whispered, her eyes darting to the parking lot and sidewalk around them.

She squared her shoulders in what appeared to be an attempt to regain her composure and pulled open the door to the building.

The three of them moved through the building's lobby silently. Sarah let them into her office and through the waiting area to her private office.

She dropped her purse next to her desk carelessly and flopped into her desk chair.

Olivia lowered herself into one of the two visitor chairs facing the desk, and Tyson took the seat beside her. Her fingers twitched against the armrests, her body vibrating with the need to demand answers. But she forced herself to remain quiet. Pressing might cause Sarah to retreat back behind her professional walls. The seconds stretched.

Tyson broke the silence. "Did you know Waldo Emerson Sr. was the attorney facilitating the adoption of Annalise's baby?" His voice was gentle but direct, offering Sarah a specific thread to follow rather than leaving her to determine where to begin.

Sarah nodded, her gaze fixed on her desk. "Yes. He was the one who made the arrangements for Annalise to get to New York and provided for her while she was there."

Olivia leaned forward, her heartbeat quickening. This confirmed what they had begun to suspect, but hearing it stated so plainly made it real in a way their speculations hadn't been. Waldo Emerson Sr. had been involved in her adoption. Had known who she was. Had known her birth father.

Sarah met Olivia's gaze. "I didn't lie to you. I don't know who the father of Annalise's baby is."

Olivia's focus narrowed on Sarah's face, searching desperately for some sign that this was another evasion, another half-truth. But she saw only resignation there, not deception.

Her throat tightened. After everything—the DNA test, tracking down Sarah, Waldo Emerson's murder—to still not know who her father was seemed like a cruel blow. Her emotions swirled like water circling a drain, desperation and frustration.

A warm pressure on her hand startled her back to the present. Tyson had reached across the space between their chairs to grasp her fingers. The contact was brief, a quick squeeze before he withdrew, but it anchored her, pulling her back from the edge of her spiraling thoughts.

Sarah continued speaking. "Annalise initially agreed to put her baby up for adoption." Her eyes flitted to Olivia for the briefest moment before returning to Tyson.

A flare of irritation went through Olivia at being so pointedly ignored. *Let her talk.* As long as Sarah was talking, Olivia didn't care if she pretended she wasn't there.

"We spoke every day while she was in New York," Sarah said, "and although she was afraid of giving birth, she thought she was doing the right thing. She knew she couldn't give a baby the life it deserved. Not at nineteen with only a high school education and especially not with the father so adamant that he not be involved."

Even though she'd seen how much effort her birth father had gone through to remain anonymous, it was painful to hear how "adamant" he'd been about not being involved with her. She had been unwanted by him from the very beginning. The knowledge settled like a stone in her stomach.

Tyson leaned forward, his elbows resting on his knees. "So, the baby's father did pay for her stay in New York and the adoption."

"Yes. He paid for and arranged it all." Sarah's voice grew steadier. "An apartment in New York for months, someone to check in on Annalise. The hospital, and birth, and the adoption. All of it." Her fingers traced invisible patterns on her desk blotter. "He even tried to give Annalise some money so she could start a new life in New York or anywhere else. I don't think he wanted her to come back to Galesburg, but Annalise refused to stay in New York."

Olivia absorbed these details with a growing sense of disorientation. Her father had orchestrated an elaborate plan to hide both the pregnancy and the baby that came of it. The precision of the arrangements suggested not just wealth but a methodical mind, someone accustomed to solving problems efficiently.

Sarah laughed suddenly, a sound devoid of humor that scraped against Olivia's nerves. "I think part of Annalise thought that they would pick up where they left off when she got back after the baby was born."

The pity in Sarah's voice made Olivia wince. She could imagine her young mother, heartbroken but hopeful, returning to Galesburg with expectations that would surely be crushed. There was something both tragic and admirable in that kind of persistent hope. An unexpected surge of tenderness toward the woman who had given birth to her went through her.

Tyson slid a look at Olivia before asking his next question, a brief glance that seemed to check whether she was steady enough to hear more. She appreciated the concern but met his eyes with what she hoped was reassuring firmness. She needed to know everything, no matter how painful.

"Did they pick up the affair again when Annalise returned?" Tyson's question was gentle but direct.

Sarah sighed deeply, her shoulders slumping as if the weight of old disappointments still pressed upon them. She nodded shallowly, the motion barely perceptible. "Yes. I told Annalise she should move on. That she deserved more. A man who was single and wanted a life with her."

Sarah's face contorted into a scowl, lines deepening around her mouth. "Married men never leave their wives."

Those five words landed with such bitter conviction that Olivia immediately sensed a personal story behind them. Sarah's eyes glazed over. Olivia wondered if Sarah too had once waited for a married man to choose her, had nurtured the same impossible hopes as Annalise. It would explain her investment in Annalise's situation, maybe even her reluctance to speak about it now.

Sarah's expression softened into sadness. "Annalise wouldn't hear it. She was so sure that this was her soulmate. She even…" Her voice trailed off, hesitation evident in the sudden tension around her mouth.

"She even what?" Olivia couldn't stop herself from prompting.

For the first time since they'd entered the office, Sarah looked directly at Olivia. "Annalise started talking about getting her child back. About becoming a family, her, the father and their child." The words came faster now, urgent. "I tried—" Sarah's voice cracked with a desperation that seemed to reach across decades "—to get through to her. But she was so sure that if she just got the baby back, he'd come around."

Olivia's heart stuttered in her chest, tears pressing hot against the back of her eyes. "My mother wanted me back." Her voice sounded strange to her own ears, suffused with wonder and a fragile kind of joy.

Sarah's eyes widened, maybe surprised by the naked emotion in Olivia's voice.

"I got the DNA test results," Olivia added, the words tumbling out before she could consider them. "I am Annalise's daughter."

Tears welled in Sarah's eyes. "You look exactly like Annalise." She sniffled and pulled a tissue from the box on her desk, dabbing at her eyes with unsteady fingers.

"Is there anything else you can tell us that might help us locate Olivia's birth father?" Tyson asked.

Sarah blew her nose and seemed to consider the question, her gaze turning inward. "It was a long time ago, but seeing you the other day—" she looked at Olivia again with that same recognition "—brought back memories I hadn't thought about for decades. I recalled that Annalise said she and her lover used to meet at his cabin off Route 360."

A cabin, a physical location tied to her father. It was concrete, traceable, a thread they could follow. For the first time since learning about Waldo Emerson's death, she'd had a glimmer of real hope.

But when she glanced at Tyson, his expression didn't mirror her excitement. His face remained carefully neutral, his posture unchanged. "Off Route 360. That's all she said."

Sarah nodded and spread her hands in a gesture of apology. "I'm sorry. That's all I remember."

A buzzing sound interrupted the moment, and Sarah looked over the tops of Tyson's and Olivia's heads toward the door. Olivia turned in her chair and noticed a light above the doorway had illuminated, pulsing gently.

"I'm sorry. My client is here." Sarah stood, smoothing her skirt with practiced hands that had regained their steadiness.

Tyson rose to his feet, and Olivia followed suit, feeling oddly reluctant to leave this room where so many secrets had finally been spoken aloud. It felt like leaving in the middle of a story.

"If you remember anything else, don't hesitate to call me," Tyson said, handing Sarah his card even though she surely already had his contact information.

Sarah nodded, her professional demeanor back in place.

Olivia followed Tyson out of the office, and through the

building's lobby. She blinked against the sudden brightness of the afternoon sun.

One thought pushed through the tangle of emotions, bright with possibility. The cabin. A tangible connection to her birth father.

"Hey." She grabbed Tyson's arm, the impulse to touch him, to anchor herself amid the whirl of her thoughts. "Why aren't you more excited? Sarah gave us a lead. We can find out who owned a cabin off Route 360 and narrow down who my father could be."

Tyson sighed, his eyes held a warmth that softened what came next. "Route 360 runs for miles. And there are several named roads that shoot off it and even more unnamed roads. There could be a hundred cabins."

In her mind, "a cabin off Route 360" had seemed specific, almost like an address. Now she pictured a winding highway cutting through forests and fields, countless turnoffs leading to secluded properties hidden among the trees. Some of her excitement dimmed.

"It is a lead and we'll follow it," Tyson added, his tone becoming more encouraging. "No matter how secretive people think they're being, they always leave clues. Someone always sees something. We just need to find out who and what."

She appreciated his attempt to revive her spirits, but logic had reasserted itself in her mind. "What and who thirty years later," she said dejectedly.

Three decades of dust had settled over whatever traces her father might have left behind. Memories would have faded, records might have been destroyed or lost, witnesses moved away or died. The cabin itself could have been sold multiple times or torn down entirely.

Tyson leaned down, bringing his face level with hers, close enough that she could see the fine lines at the corners of his eyes. The sudden proximity sent a jolt through her system, not unpleasant, but unexpected.

"Hey," he said softly. "We've come this far. We'll figure this out."

The alternative, giving up, accepting that she might never know her father's identity, was unthinkable.

Tyson straightened, the moment of intimate connection passing. "I've got to get back to the station," he said, checking his watch with a frown. "But I can drop you off at your rental on the way."

They would find that cabin and uncover her father's identity.

Chapter Seventeen

The dashboard clock read 8:30 p.m. when he killed the engine. He'd parked his sedan on the unlit stretch of asphalt behind Amelia's Café, positioned between two dumpsters where the shadows pooled thick and impenetrable. Fifteen minutes had passed since the neon Open sign flickered off. A light burned through the window of the kitchen. Amelia's car was parked in the smaller, rear lot in the spot nearest to the back door of the café.

His fingers drummed against the steering wheel, each tap sending small vibrations up his arm. A thin sheen of sweat coated his palms despite the evening chill. He wiped them on his jeans, leaving damp streaks on the denim. A piece of wood rested on the passenger seat beside him.

He'd gone inside just an hour ago and ordered a cappuccino he'd barely tasted.

"You need anything else?" she'd asked, smiling at him. He'd shaken his head, marveling at how similar her voice was to Annalise's.

Amelia had never given any indication that she knew he was the father of Annalise's baby. But he just couldn't take the chance. What if Annalise had confided in her sister? Now that Olivia had come around, kicking up long buried memories, Amelia might remember something—a phone call, a letter, a passing comment—that connected him to Annalise.

I'm sorry, he thought, sending it silently to Amelia as he'd left the café, determined to wait for her in his car.

The security camera that monitored the back entrance now hung limp against the wall, its wires neatly severed an hour before closing. No witnesses, no footage. A simple robbery gone wrong. That's what the police would see. Take her purse. Leave no evidence.

His eyes drifted to the piece of lumber he'd taken from a construction site dumpster a block away. No connection to him, no fingerprints to worry about, and it looked like a weapon of opportunity. Something a burglar might have found in the back alley behind the café and grabbed in the moment.

The back door of the café swung open, spilling yellow light across the pavement. Amelia appeared, one hand clutching a bulging garbage bag, the other holding her purse. Her hair was tied back in a loose ponytail, and she moved with the heavy steps of someone at the end of a long shift.

His heart slammed against his ribs. *Just get out and get it done.*

He slid out of the car, easing the door shut with barely a click. Twenty yards separated him from Amelia, who'd set down the garbage bag and was now fumbling with her keys, her back to him.

Gravel crunched under his shoes as he moved forward, each step deliberate and measured. The night air pressed cold against his face. His breathing sounded thunderous in his ears, though he knew it was barely audible.

Amelia dropped her keys and cursed softly, bending to retrieve them. The movement saved her from seeing his approach in her peripheral vision. He quickened his pace.

She straightened, inserted the key into the lock and began to turn. Something, some protective instinct, made her turn toward him.

He swung.

The sound was both duller and louder than he'd expected. A sick thud followed by a cracking noise that rippled up his arms. Amelia didn't cry out. Her body simply crumpled, folding at the knees as if her strings had been cut. Her purse slipped from her fingers and landed beside her with a soft thump. She lay sprawled on the concrete, one arm twisted beneath her, her ponytail fanned out like spilled ink.

A dark puddle of blood spread around her head. The sight of it froze him in place. He couldn't tell if she was breathing. Her chest didn't appear to be moving, but his own pulse was hammering so loudly he couldn't focus. He took a half step closer, then stopped. Her face was turned away from him, but he could see the gash where the wood had connected with her skull.

His stomach lurched. Bile rose hot and bitter in his throat, and he swallowed it down with a choked sound. This wasn't like before. When he'd killed Waldo, it had been almost mechanical, a problem to solve, an inconvenience to eliminate. He'd barely known the man, and Waldo had been blackmailing him. His death had felt justified, even necessary.

But Amelia… Amelia was different. He knew the pitch of her laugh, the way she hummed while she worked, how she always gave free cookies to the kids who came to the café with their parents. She'd never done anything to him. Never threatened him. Had never even looked at him with suspicion.

And now she lay bleeding at his feet.

"I had to," he whispered, though no one was there to hear his justification. "I had to be sure."

The wood slipped from his fingers and clattered to the ground beside her. He should go inside now, ransack the register, make it look like the robbery he'd planned. But his legs carried him backward, away from the spreading pool of blood, away from the still form on the concrete.

Panic surged through him. He turned and ran, his footfalls suddenly deafening in the quiet night. He reached his car and wrenched the door open, throwing himself inside with none of the caution he'd shown earlier.

"Stupid, stupid, stupid!" He slammed his fist against the steering wheel once, twice, a third time. The horn blared on the final impact, the sound cutting through the night like an alarm. He froze, then jammed the car into Drive and pressed the gas pedal to the floor.

The tires squealed as he tore away, putting distance between himself and what he'd done.

Chapter Eighteen

Tyson leaned back in his chair, rubbing his eyes until colored spots danced behind his lids. Waldo Emerson's murder file lay open before him, a messy constellation of interviews, evidence and half-formed theories. He'd spent the entire day traversing the town, speaking to everyone who knew the lawyer. A pinched-faced ex-wife who didn't appear at all broken up by the murder of her ex-husband, lawyers in expensive suits and a handful of friends who seemed like the only people who would really miss Waldo. It was exhausting work, but his mind refused to quiet, circling back to one persistent thought. Olivia could be in danger. That thought twisted something primal inside him.

He flipped through his notes again. Waldo had made enemies, as any good lawyer should. Emerson & Associates was primarily a family law practice. Waldo had worked on numerous nasty divorces, and there was a long-running feud with Judge Manesha Carlton over a ruling three years back. An estate dispute over a family company. Solid leads that he'd have to pursue.

But his gut told him that Waldo hadn't been killed over grudges or courtroom dramatics. The timing was too aligned with Olivia's return to Galesburg. Waldo had known something about the identity of Olivia's father. Knowledge that had led to his death.

His phone sat heavy in his pocket. His fingers itched to dial Olivia's number, to hear her voice and confirm she was safe.

"Get a grip," he muttered to himself.

The digital clock on his monitor read 8:50 p.m. He'd forgotten to eat dinner.

"Damn it." He sighed, his stomach punctuating the sentiment with a low growl. In LA, he could have found food at any hour. Here, almost everything would be locked up tight.

He stood, stretching until his spine cracked. The movement sent a dull ache across his shoulders, reminding him he wasn't as young as he used to be. But hungry was hungry, and he remembered Amelia often worked late at the café preparing for the next day.

The bullpen stretched before him, desks empty except for the night shift. Officer Martinez typed up a report with two fingers, and Officer Dawes read on his phone, his feet propped on his desk. The fluorescent lights cast everything in a sickly glow, making the institutional beige walls look jaundiced.

"Going somewhere, Chief?" Martinez asked, looking up from her hunt-and-peck typing.

"Just stretching my legs," he replied, grabbing his jacket from the back of his chair. "Thought I'd walk over to Amelia's, see if she's got any pie left."

Dawes snorted without looking up from his phone. "Good luck. Walked by there thirty minutes ago and she was closing up."

Tyson shrugged. "Worth a shot. Call if anything comes in."

"Will do, Chief," Martinez said, her dark eyes lingering on his face a moment too long. "You look beat. Maybe go home and grab some sleep after you get your pie. We've got things under control for the night."

He forced a smile before making his way out of the police station.

The night air hit him like a cold slap as he stepped outside, and Tyson welcomed it. The autumn chill cleared his head, swept away the cobwebs of fatigue and the thoughts of Olivia. He turned toward Main Street, his steps echoing on the empty sidewalk. A single car passed, headlights sweeping over him before leaving him in darkness again.

He shoved his hands in his pockets and walked faster, trying to outpace his own thoughts. He couldn't shake the feeling that time was running out. For the case. For Olivia. For all of them. There was a killer somewhere in Galesburg. And he had the sinking feeling that Waldo may have been just the beginning.

He'd pulled a list of cabins off Route 360 from real estate records. Eighty-seven cabins. He'd printed out the list, the paper now folded and soft-edged in his pocket from being handled throughout the day. Eighty-seven possible locations where Annalise had conceived her daughter, where a secret had been born that was worth killing for thirty years later.

He ran the numbers in his head again, the familiar calculation of a detective breaking down an impossible task into manageable pieces. He'd eliminated twenty-three properties that weren't built until after Olivia's conception. That still left sixty-four cabins, sixty-four potential owners who might be Olivia's father.

The real problem was that they couldn't just look at current owners. People sold properties, passed them down to children, lost them in divorces. He needed historical records, ownership chains that stretched back three decades. And even then, he couldn't be certain the cabin had belonged to Annalise's lover. It might have been a friend's place, a relative's getaway, or even a rental.

He'd set Officer Revis on the background checks. The kid had looked excited at first, the way rookies always did when given real detective work. His enthusiasm had faded when Tyson explained the scope, a detailed background on each male property owner, focusing on marital status thirty years ago, connections to Annalise or her family, history of violence.

"It'll take days, Chief," Revis had said, looking overwhelmed.

"Then you better get started," Tyson had replied, not unkindly. It would take days, maybe weeks, and even then they might find nothing. A three-decade-old affair left few traces, especially if the man had been careful. And he must have been, to have kept his identity secret all these years.

His stomach twisted with hunger. He'd skipped lunch, too caught up in interviews to notice the time, and breakfast had been nothing but coffee and half a stale doughnut.

The outline of Amelia's Café appeared ahead, a squat brick building with wide windows. No welcoming lights spilled onto the sidewalk. No smell of coffee or baking bread. Just darkness, and the sign in the window turned to Closed.

"Damn it," Tyson muttered, stopping short. He pressed his face to the glass, cupping his hands around his eyes to peer inside. The chairs were up on the tables, the floor freshly mopped. Not a soul in sight.

His stomach complained loudly, the sound obscenely noisy in the quiet street. He checked his watch: 9:03 p.m. Too late for anywhere else in this town. He could go back to the station, choke down a sandwich from the vending machine, but the thought of those stale chips and cardboard cookies was worse than the hunger in his stomach.

He could go home and try to get some sleep. Start fresh in the morning. But something stopped him. A feeling, settling at the base of his spine. The hair on his arms stood up. He'd been a cop too long, and served in the military before that, to ignore the feeling. It had saved his life more than once.

He walked around the corner to the back lot, his hand resting on his service weapon.

Amelia's blue Taurus sat alone. His eyes swept the lot methodically, the dumpsters against the far wall, recycling bins, the back door to the café standing ajar. And on the ground in front of the door, a dark mass. His stomach dropped as he drew his gun, thumbing off the safety, eyes scanning the shadows for movement.

Ten feet from the door, he could make out the green apron Amelia always wore and a sweep of silver-gray hair.

"Amelia?" His voice cracked on her name.

No answer. Tyson covered the remaining distance at a run, still scanning the area, dividing his attention between the potential threat and the crumpled figure.

He reached her side, crouching low. Amelia lay on her side, her body curled inward like a child's. Her silver-gray hair spilled across her face, matted with blood.

"Amelia," he said again, gentler this time. He reached out, fingers searching for a pulse at her neck while his other hand pulled his phone from his pocket. His fingers found the faint, thready pulse beneath her jaw.

Somewhere in the distance, a car horn sounded.

"Amelia! Amelia! Can you hear me?" He shifted to see her face, brushing the hair back gently. A gash ran across her forehead. Her eyes remained closed, lips parted, no response to his voice.

His phone finally connected, and he didn't wait for the officer to finish the standard greeting.

"This is the Chief Morrow. I need an ambulance behind Amelia's Café now. Amelia's down, badly hurt. Possible assault. Tell them to hurry." His voice came out harder than he intended, clipped and fierce.

"Yes, sir," came Martinez's steady reply. "Ambulance dispatched. Do you need backup?"

"Yes. Full response."

He ended the call and turned back to Amelia, holstering his gun to free both hands. Gently, he checked for other injuries.

"Amelia, it's Tyson. I'm here. Stay with me." He pulled off his jacket, folding it carefully beneath her head as a cushion. "Help is coming. Just hold on."

Her eyelids fluttered, the barest movement, gone so quickly he might have imagined it. But it was a sign of life, and he clung to it.

"That's it, Amelia. Fight. You hear me? You fight." His voice cracked again, and he didn't try to steady it.

In the distance, sirens wailed. Tyson took Amelia's hand.

"I'll find who did this," he promised, the words barely audible beneath the approaching sirens. "And they will pay."

Chapter Nineteen

Olivia burst through the hospital doors, the antiseptic smell wrapping around her like blanket. She'd thrown jeans over her pajama shorts and hadn't even bothered changing out of her sleep top before hopping into her car after Stephanie's panicked call about Amelia's assault. The harsh fluorescent lights of Montville Hospital's entrance stung, and it took a moment for her eyes adjust. When they did, she spotted Stephanie, Geo, Tom, Marcus and Tyson huddled in the waiting area, their faces drawn with worry.

She rushed toward them.

"How is Amelia?" she asked, breathless from her dash from the parking lot.

Stephanie's eyes were swollen and red-rimmed and her cheeks blotchy from tears. She clung to Geo with white-knuckled fingers. "We don't know anything," she said, her voice thin and scratchy. "The doctors are looking at her now."

Olivia's stomach twisted.

Geo slipped an arm around Stephanie's shoulders, his face etched with concern not just for Amelia, but for his wife. "Stephanie, let's have a seat. It could take a while before we know anything."

He guided her to the nearest chair, and Stephanie folded into it.

"How about I go get us all coffee?" Marcus suggested,

his voice cutting through the heavy silence that had settled over them.

Tom stood nearby, his fingers fidgeting with the hem of his shirt. His face was pale, under the fluorescent lights. "I'll… I'll help. I can't just stand around doing nothing."

Marcus turned to him with understanding in his eyes. He reached out and clapped Tom on the shoulder. "Good idea."

The two men walked away down the hallway, their footsteps fading into the background hum of distant hospital machinery.

"You didn't need to rush over," Tyson said quietly, his voice rough around the edges.

She looked up into his eyes, noting the dark circles beneath them, and the tension in his jaw. "Of course I did. I wanted to be here for Stephanie." She reached out and took his hand, feeling the slight tremble in his fingers that his otherwise composed demeanor concealed. His skin was cool against hers, and she resisted the urge to bring his hand to her lips. "And for you."

Tyson leaned his shoulder into hers, the gesture more intimate than words.

"How are you doing?"

"I found her," he said. "I rode to the hospital in the ambulance with her." His voice cracked. "Olivia, it's bad."

His Adam's apple bobbed as he swallowed hard, fighting back tears. "If I lose her…" The sentence hung unfinished, too painful to complete.

She didn't care who might see or what they might think. She wrapped her arms around Tyson, pulling him close, feeling his heart beat against her chest. "Amelia is strong. You aren't going to lose her."

Tyson's arms went around her, and he held her as if she were the only thing keeping him from completely falling apart.

Olivia closed her eyes, breathing him in. The tension in his shoulders eased. She didn't know how long they stood like that before the sound of approaching footsteps broke the spell.

They pulled apart just as a doctor in blue scrubs walked into the waiting room. She kept her hand on Tyson's arm, feeling the muscles tense beneath her fingers as they both turned toward the doctor. Stephanie and Geo looked up from where they sat, Stephanie's face a mask of desperate hope and terrible fear.

"I'm looking for the family of Amelia Farr," the doctor announced, his voice cutting through the waiting room's heavy silence. Tyson stiffened beside her.

Stephanie bolted upright from her chair. "I'm her daughter," Stephanie said, her voice trembling like a leaf in autumn. "And this is my husband." She gestured to Geo, who stood protectively at her side.

"I'm Dr. Anderson," he said, his voice measured and professional. "I've treated your mother in the ER. She has sustained a worrisome head injury."

Olivia tightened her grip on Tyson's hand, feeling his pulse hammering through his fingers.

"Her skull fracture is very serious," the doctor continued. "We've put her in an induced coma to give the swelling time to go down."

Stephanie made a small, broken sound. Geo wrapped an arm around her shoulders, pulling her close. The fluorescent lights seemed to bleach all color from Stephanie's face, leaving her looking ghostlike.

"The next forty-eight hours will be crucial," Dr. Anderson said, his eyes moving between their faces. "I suggest you all go home and get some rest."

Stephanie turned and buried her face against Geo's chest, her shoulders shaking with silent sobs. Geo cradled her head, his fingers threading through her hair with practiced tenderness.

Tyson's hand slipped from hers, the sudden absence of his touch leaving her fingers cold. He stepped forward, intercepting the doctor as he turned to leave.

"Doctor," Tyson said, his voice authoritative, "I'm Chief Tyson Morrow. I'll be investigating this case as an assault."

The word *assault* hung in the air, sharp-edged and ugly. This wasn't an accident. Someone had deliberately hurt Amelia.

Dr. Anderson nodded, his expression grave. "Good. It appears that Ms. Farr was hit in the head with a blunt instrument. I'll make sure you get her clothes and personal effects and whatever other information you need. I hope you catch whoever did this, and quickly."

Olivia moved back to Tyson's side, taking his hand again. His skin was colder now.

"Let me take you home," she said, noticing the exhaustion etched into the lines around his eyes.

Tyson shook his head. "I should stay."

"You heard the doctor," she countered gently. She reached up with her free hand and touched his cheek, a brief, tender gesture. "There's nothing you can do for Amelia here, and you look like you're about to fall down." She softened her words with a small, sad smile. "You won't be able to help anyone if you don't take care of yourself."

He nodded reluctantly, his eyes still fixed on the hallway where the doctor had disappeared, as if he might somehow see through the walls to where Amelia lay.

They moved together toward Stephanie and Geo. Stephanie had composed herself somewhat, but she still leaned heavily on Geo, as if standing upright required more strength than she possessed.

"We're going to head out," she said, hating how inadequate the words were in the face of Stephanie's pain. "Call if you need anything at all, day or night."

Stephanie nodded, reaching out to squeeze her arm. "Thank you for coming," she whispered.

"I'll be back first thing in the morning," Tyson said. "And I'll have officers looking into this immediately."

The promise seemed to give Stephanie a measure of comfort. She nodded again, then turned back to Geo, who led her gently to the chairs.

They turned and almost collided with Tom and Marcus returning with cardboard trays of coffee cups.

They waited while Stephanie, now seated again with Geo beside her, recounted the doctor's words. Tom's face crumpled with concern. Marcus remained stoic, his hand resting supportively on Tom's shoulder.

"I'll take care of making sure the café remains closed," Tom assured Stephanie, his voice steadier than his expression. "I'll post a sign that it will be closed indefinitely."

Stephanie managed a fragile smile, reaching into her purse for the café keys. She pressed them into Tom's hand, then rose on tiptoe to kiss his cheek. "Thank you."

With final nods of goodbye, Olivia and Tyson made their way out of the hospital. The weight of the night's events weighed on her. Tyson moved like a man underwater, his stride slowed by exhaustion and grief.

She guided her car through the empty streets, Tyson sitting beside her in silence, both of them lost in their own thoughts. The hospital was nearly a forty-minute drive from Galesburg, and the next time she glanced over at Tyson his head had tilted against the window, eyes closed, his breathing deepened into the rhythm of sleep, the tension drained from his face. She returned her gaze to the road, allowing him this brief escape into unconsciousness.

The familiar contours of the lake emerged and she turned onto the narrow road that led to the rental house, the car's headlights cutting through the trees that lined the driveway.

She pulled up in front of the lake house and turned off the engine. The sudden silence seemed to press against her eardrums. Tyson didn't stir. She took a moment to study him in the moonlight that filtered through the windshield, the stubble darkening his jaw, the way his eyelashes cast shadows on his cheeks, the slight part of his lips as he breathed.

"Tyson," she said, placing a gentle hand on his arm. "We're here."

He woke instantly, blinking and straightening in his seat. "I'm sorry," he said, his voice gravelly with sleep. "I didn't mean to doze off."

He looked out the window. "I should have called a car to take me home," he said, reaching for his phone in his pocket. "I can call for one now."

Her hand covered his, stilling the movement. "No. I have a guest room. Two actually." Her voice was soft but firm. "You can sleep here for the night."

The moonlight was full and bright, illuminating Tyson's face with a silvery glow. She could see every line, every shadow, the weariness in his eyes and hesitation.

"Are you sure?" he asked.

"Yes. It's fine. You should get in bed as soon as possible." Heat rose to her cheeks as she realized how they might sound. "I mean you should go to sleep. It's been a long day."

Tyson chuckled, the sound low and warm in the confined space of the car. "I understand what you mean." He glanced out the window toward the lake house's front door, his expression shifting, becoming more serious. "It might not be a bad idea for me to stay here."

The change in his tone sent a chill down her spine. It wasn't just about convenience or exhaustion anymore. She studied his face, reading the concern etched there.

"You think the same person who killed Waldo attacked Amelia, don't you," she said. It wasn't a question.

Tyson turned back toward her, his eyes meeting hers in the dim light. "Yes. I do."

She let out a rugged breath, the implications of his words sinking in. "And you think he'll come after me next."

The car suddenly felt intimate. Tyson reached across the console and took her hand, pulling her gently toward him until their foreheads met. The warmth of his skin against hers was both comforting and electric.

"I won't let anything happen to you," he said, his voice a low, fierce promise that vibrated through her.

Her heart thundered in her chest. She closed the distance between them and kissed him lightly. But what began as gentle quickly transformed as Tyson responded, his hand moving to cup the back of her neck, drawing her closer, and she folded into him.

The kiss deepened, becoming urgent, hungry. Heat bloomed in her chest and spread through her body like wildfire. His lips were insistent against hers, his breath warm on her skin. She was pulled into a current of desire that had been building since their first meeting.

His other hand found her waist, fingers pressing through the thin fabric of her pajama top. She leaned into his touch, the center console digging uncomfortably into her side, but she hardly noticed, lost in the sensation of his mouth on hers, the taste of him, the scent of his skin.

The world outside the car faded away until there was only the two of them, wrapped in moonlight.

Her breath came in short gasps when they finally broke apart. She met Tyson's gaze and found a question in his eyes. She smiled and nodded. Their lips met again in a kiss even more fevered than before, his hands threading through her hair, her fingers gripping the front of his shirt.

Tyson's mouth moved from her lips to her neck, trailing fire along her skin. She tilted her head back, a soft laugh escaping her as pleasure coursed through her body.

"You know there's an entire house right there," she said, her voice husky with desire. "And even though I don't really have neighbors here, we might want to take this inside."

Tyson growled against her throat, the vibration sending shivers down her spine. He pulled away reluctantly, his eyes dark and hungry in the moonlight. The cool night air rushed into the space between them.

They exited the car with an urgency that made her fumble with her keys. Her body thrummed with anticipation, with need. Her hands trembled as she fitted the key into the lock. She could feel Tyson behind her, the heat of his body, his breath warm against her neck. The proximity was intoxicating, making it difficult to focus on the simple task of unlocking her door.

The lock gave way with a click. They stepped inside, and she turned to face Tyson, suddenly aware of the rapid beating of her heart, the rise and fall of her chest. There was a moment of suspended time as they stood looking at each other across the entryway, a heartbeat of anticipation before Tyson closed the distance between them. His hands found her waist, drawing her against him as his lips sought her neck once more. Her eyes fluttered closed at the sensation of his mouth on her skin, the gentle scrape of his stubble, the heat of his breath.

"We don't have to do this if you aren't sure," he said against her collarbone, his voice rough with restraint. "I can still call a car to pick me up."

She pulled back just enough to look into his eyes. In the dim light, his face was all planes and shadows, beautiful in its intensity. She placed her palm against his cheek, feeling the warmth of his skin, the slight tremor in his jaw that betrayed his effort at control.

"No," she said firmly. "I want this." She took a breath, her thumb tracing the curve of his lower lip. "I've wanted this since you showed up at my door the night I got to town."

Something shifted in Tyson's expression. He growled, a primal sound that stirred something deep inside her, and captured her mouth with his. The kiss was different now, charged with the knowledge that there would be no more hesitation, no more holding back.

His hands were everywhere. Sliding under her pajama top, tracing the curve of her spine, pulling her hips against his. She responded in kind, fingers working at the buttons of his shirt, desperate to feel his skin against hers.

They moved together toward the living room, a stumbling dance of desire, unwilling to break contact even for the few steps it took to reach their destination.

Her legs hit the sofa, and Tyson followed her down onto the cushions, his weight a delicious pressure that anchored her to the moment. The lamp's glow caught the planes of his chest as she pushed his shirt from his shoulders, revealing the contours of muscle and the scattered scars that told stories she would ask about someday, but not now.

Now there was only the heat of his mouth on her skin. The gentle pressure of his hands guiding her pajama top over her head. The shock of cool air against her exposed flesh quickly replaced by the warmth of his touch. She arched into him, a soft sound of pleasure escaping her lips as his fingers traced patterns of desire across her body.

With the lake water lapping gently at the shore outside, time seemed to slow and stretch as they explored each other. Tyson whispered her name against her skin like a prayer, and she responded with soft sounds of encouragement, her hands mapping the planes of his back, the curve of his shoulders. The sofa beneath them was narrow, forcing them to press close.

Afterward, they lay tangled together on the sofa, Tyson's arm curved protectively around her waist, her head nestled against his chest where she could hear the steady beat of his heart.

For now, the dangers waiting beyond the lake house doors seemed distant and dim, so she closed her eyes and slept.

Chapter Twenty

Sunlight streamed through the half-closed blinds, painting warm stripes across Olivia's face. She stretched beneath the sheets. Fragments of the previous night flickered through her mind. Tyson's hands on her skin, his breath against her neck, their bodies intertwined first on the sofa and later in this very bed. She smiled, eyes still closed, and reached across the mattress expecting to find his warmth. Her fingers met only cool, empty sheets.

Her eyes fluttered open. The indentation where Tyson's head had rested on the pillow remained, but he was gone. A folded piece of paper sat on the nightstand, her name scrawled across it in a hasty, slanting script. She propped herself up on one elbow and unfolded the note.

"Had to go home to change, then straight to work. We're stretched thin, but I'll have an officer drive by regularly. Call you later. Tyson."

She set the note aside and sank back into her pillow, replaying moments from the night before. Their connection had been unexpected but undeniable. She didn't regret it, quite the opposite. Her body still hummed with the memory of his touch. But she needed to make sure he understood this was casual. She couldn't offer more, not when her life waited for her hundreds of miles away.

Or did it? Stephanie's request that she stay in Galesburg

tickled at the edges of her thoughts. She stared at the ceiling, considering the possibility for the first time without immediately dismissing it. Her business was in DC, yes, but her work was increasingly virtual. Most clients she served remotely, sending designs and revisions back and forth online. She rarely met anyone face-to-face anymore.

"Stop it," she whispered to the empty room. "You're getting ahead of yourself."

She swung her legs over the side of the bed and sat up. One night with Tyson and suddenly she was contemplating uprooting her entire life? That wasn't like her. She needed to focus on why she'd come to Galesburg in the first place. To learn who her birth father was.

A pang of guilt stabbed through her chest as her thoughts turned to Amelia. A man was dead, and Amelia lay unconscious in a hospital bed because Olivia had come asking questions about the past.

She shook her head firmly. "No. The only person responsible for violence is the person who commits it." Still, the guilt lingered.

She pushed herself to her feet and padded to the bathroom. The shower's hot water beat against her skin, washing away the last traces of sleep. She tried to focus on what she needed to get done that morning. Visiting Amelia, supporting Stephanie and finding out what Tyson had learned about the attack. Her mind kept circling back to Tyson, to the weight of his arms around her, to the question of what came next.

An hour and a half later, she pulled into the hospital parking lot and made her way to the waiting room. Stephanie sat hunched in a chair. Dark circles shadowed her eyes, but she looked up when she entered, her exhausted face brightening.

"You came," Stephanie said, standing to embrace her. The

hug was tight, desperate, and she found herself blinking back unexpected tears.

"Of course I did," she replied, pulling back to study Stephanie's face. "How are you holding up?"

Stephanie shrugged, her shoulders slumping. "I'm okay. Just worried sick. Geo stayed home with Hanes today. We kept him out of preschool—we're worried about his safety after what happened."

She nodded, understanding blooming in her chest. "That makes sense."

"Geo wants us to leave town," Stephanie whispered. "To go somewhere safe, not tell anyone where we are. But I can't leave Mom like this." Her voice cracked on the last word.

She squeezed Stephanie's hand. "If there's anything I can do, anything at all, just let me know."

A small, tired smile curved Stephanie's lips. "You're doing it. Just by being here." She gestured toward the hallway. "Want to see her?"

Olivia nodded, and Stephanie led the way to Amelia's room. The steady beep of monitors greeted them as they entered. Tears pricked at her eyes at the sight of Amelia in the hospital bed, tubes and wires connecting her to various machines. Her skin was ashen and she looked fragile, nothing like the fierce woman who had stubbornly refused to tell her about her birth mother just days ago.

Stephanie moved to the chair closest to the bed, taking her mother's limp hand between her own. Olivia settled into a chair on the opposite side of the hospital bed, unsure what to do or say.

"The doctors say her vital signs are stable," Stephanie said, her eyes fixed on Amelia's face. "But they don't know when she'll wake up. If…" She swallowed hard. "If she'll wake up."

She reached across the bed to touch Stephanie's arm. "She's strong. I haven't known her long, but that much is obvious."

Stephanie nodded, blinking rapidly. "She is. The strongest person I know."

They fell silent again, the weight of the situation settling around them like a heavy blanket. Who had done this? Why? Was it truly connected to her arrival? To the secrets of the past she'd been trying to unearth?

The minutes stretched, marked only by the steady electronic heartbeat and the occasional squeak of rubber-soled shoes passing in the hallway.

The door to Amelia's room swung open with a soft whoosh, drawing her attention from Amelia's still form. Tyson stood in the doorway, a bouquet of bright flowers in one hand, his police badge visible on his belt. His eyes found her first, his gaze sliding over her with a mixture of hesitation and heat that made her skin prickle despite the clinical chill of the hospital room. The memory of his hands on her body the night before flashed unbidden through her mind, and she straightened in her chair, suddenly aware of the loose strand of hair that had fallen across her cheek.

Stephanie noticed him a moment later, her tired face brightening. Her eyes darted between them, a knowing smile tugging at the corners of her mouth. Heat rose in Olivia's cheeks, and she busied herself with smoothing nonexistent wrinkles from her pants. Tyson crossed the room in three long strides, and Stephanie rose from her chair to let him envelope her in a one-armed hug.

"These are for you," he said, offering the bouquet. "Hoping they might cheer you up a bit."

Stephanie accepted the flowers, burying her face in the blooms for a moment. "They're beautiful. Thank you."

"How is she doing?" Tyson asked, his voice dropping as he turned toward Amelia's bed.

Stephanie cleared her throat. "No change in her condition yet. The doctors say her vitals are stable, but…" She let the sentence hang unfinished.

His jaw tightened. "I hate this."

Stephanie shook her head. "We all do."

He pulled a notebook from his back pocket. "Stephanie, I didn't want to bother you last night, but it would be helpful if I could ask you some questions now."

Stephanie straightened her shoulders, setting the flowers on the bedside table. "Anything. Anything I can do to help you find the monster that did this to my mother, I'll do."

He flipped open his notebook. "Do you know of anyone who might want to hurt Amelia? Any enemies, old grudges, recent arguments?"

Stephanie shook her head emphatically. "No. Everyone loves Mom. She's opinionated, sure, but not the kind of person who makes enemies."

"Has there been anything unusual happening at the café? Strange customers, threatening phone calls, anything out of the ordinary at all?"

Stephanie's lips quirked upward, and she cast a sidelong glance at Olivia. "Besides a long-lost cousin showing up? No."

She reached for Stephanie's hand and squeezed it, grateful for the attempt at levity in such a dark moment.

"Anyone hanging around too much? Someone who made either of you uncomfortable?" he pressed, his pen poised above the page.

Stephanie's brow furrowed in concentration. "There's a guy who comes in most mornings who always sits at the same table and stays way too long. But he's harmless, just lonely, I think. And there's a couple who argue loudly every Sunday, but they've been doing that for years." She shook her head. "Nothing that stands out as threatening."

He took their names down, then asked, "What about changes to her routine? Has Amelia been going anywhere unusual, meeting with anyone new?"

"No, she's a creature of habit. Up at five, at the café by six thirty, and she's there all day usually. Most of her social life is spent with Tom." Stephanie sighed. "The only thing different lately was her being so upset about Olivia's questions."

A fresh wave of guilt washed over her.

After a few more questions that led nowhere, he closed his notebook and tucked it away. "Stephanie, would you mind if I go to Amelia's house and take a look around? There might be something there that could help us understand what happened."

"Not at all," Stephanie replied, reaching for her purse, which sat on the floor beside her chair. "Let me find her house key."

While Stephanie dug through her bag, his eyes drifted back to Olivia. The heat in his gaze had returned, more measured now but unmistakable. The hospital room seemed to shrink around them, the space between their bodies charged with unspoken memories.

"You okay?" he asked, his voice low.

Olivia read the deeper question beneath his words. Whether she was okay with what had happened between them. Whether she regretted it in the cold light of day. She smiled, a private curve of her lips.

"Yes, I'm great," she said. "I had a very relaxing night."

The corners of his mouth twitched upward, his eyes darkening just enough to send a flutter through her stomach. The memory of his weight above her, of his breath against her neck, felt as real as if it were happening in that moment.

Stephanie stepped between them, dangling a key from her fingers. Her eyes sparkled with mischief despite her exhaustion. “I’d tell you two to get a room, but I suspect you already have.”

Embarrassment flooded Olivia’s cheeks as she jerked her gaze away from Tyson’s, fascinated by the pattern on the hospital floor tiles. She couldn’t believe how obvious it was that her relationship with him had changed.

He took the key from Stephanie with a soft chuckle, leaning in to press a quick kiss to her cheek. “You really know how to kill the mood.” He slipped the key into his pocket and turned to Olivia. “Would you like to come with me?” The question was casual, but his eyes held hers with an intensity that suggested multiple layers of meaning.

She hesitated, glancing at Amelia’s still form and then at Stephanie. “I should probably stay here with Stephanie.”

But Stephanie was already waving her off. “Go. I’ll call you if anything changes.” She settled back into the chair beside her mother’s bed, arranging the flowers in a plastic water pitcher. “Honestly, I could use a little time alone with Mom.”

She gave Stephanie a quick hug, whispering, “Call me. Anytime,” into her ear before following Tyson out the door.

Chapter Twenty-One

The Victorian house loomed before them, its weathered facade bearing the dignified weight of decades. Olivia paused at the bottom of the porch steps, a strange tightness gathering in her chest. This was Amelia's home and something about crossing this threshold felt monumental and she was entering under circumstances she wouldn't have chosen.

"Ready?" Tyson asked, his voice soft against the still afternoon air.

She nodded, swallowing the knot in her throat. "As I'll ever be."

The key turned with a solid click, and the door swung open to reveal a foyer bathed in natural light from a stained-glass window above, and gleaming hardwood floors. Her footsteps echoed in the quiet space.

She followed Tyson deeper inside, taking in the framed botanical prints lining the walls, the antique side table with a collection of ceramic birds. Little fragments of the woman she barely knew.

Tyson led her into a modern kitchen that boasted stainless-steel appliances and recessed lighting. A massive island dominated the center, its marble top cool and smooth. Copper pots hung from a ceiling rack, and glass-fronted cabinets displayed an impressive collection of dishes and specialized bakeware.

She chuckled, running her fingers along the granite island.

"This is exactly what I would have expected from someone who owns a café."

He smiled. "I spent so many hours in this kitchen, sampling her creations." His gaze took on a distant quality, like he was peering into the past. "Before she opened the café, Amelia used to run a catering business from here. The whole neighborhood would know when Amelia was testing recipes. The smells would drift all the way outside, and I'd hurry over to be her taste tester."

She tried to imagine it. Amelia surrounded by flour and spices, opening her door to neighbors. It was a version of her aunt she hoped to meet someday.

"Where should we start searching? And what should we look for?" she asked.

"Look for anything that might point to someone with a grudge against Amelia. And of course, anything, about Annalise. Or yourself," he said, leading her into what had once been a formal parlor but had been transformed into a home office.

A large oak desk faced windows that overlooked the backyard garden. Bookshelves lined the walls from floor to ceiling, their dark wood contrasting with the cream-colored walls. A comfortable-looking armchair sat in one corner, a reading lamp bent over it like a sentinel.

"I'll go through the desk," he said, settling into the chair behind it. "You take a look around."

She nodded and moved to the bookshelves, her eyes scanning the titles. The collection was vast and varied. Professional cookbooks stood in neat rows, some with spines still crisp, others worn from use, sticky notes protruding from their edges. But it was the fiction section that caught her attention. Women's fiction dominated one shelf, thrillers another and romantic comedies filled a third. Olivia pulled out a novel at random, flipping through pages marked with a coffee-stained bookmark.

Her aunt read romances. She liked thrillers. She marked her place with whatever was at hand. These details were insignificant individually but together they revealed another facet of the woman who had refused to know her. Now that she had the DNA results confirming she was Annalise's daughter, maybe Amelia would finally open up.

Behind her, she heard Tyson shuffling papers.

"Anything?" she asked, turning from the books.

He shook his head, frustration evident in the set of his shoulders. "Nothing that jumps out. It's all mundane paperwork, bills, receipts, purchase orders for the café." He held up a stack of papers. "Supply invoices, utility statements, personal bills. Nothing threatening. Nothing helpful."

She sighed, continuing her survey of the shelves.

Her gaze drifted across the rows of books, then caught on a leather-bound album wedged between two cookbooks. When she opened it, the first page was a photo of teenage Amelia and Annalise with feathered hair and brightly colored shirts, laughing into the camera.

"Tyson," she called, her voice hushed with discovery. "I think I may have found something."

The floor creaked as he abandoned his search at the desk. He came to stand behind her, close enough that his chest nearly touched her back. The heat radiating from his body sending an unexpected current of awareness racing along her skin.

Last night flooded back to her in a rush of sensory memories. Her cheeks warmed, and she fought to keep her focus on the album in her hands.

He leaned closer, his breath stirring the fine hairs at her nape. His hands settled on her shoulders, strong fingers working gently into the tense muscles there. She hadn't realized how much tension she'd been carrying until he began to release it. He bent and pressed his lips to the side of her neck. There was no passion in it, but something more tender.

Her eyes fluttered closed for a moment, surrendering to the sensation. "We should talk about what happened between us last night," she said, the words coming out before she could reconsider them.

He gave a soft groan against her skin, his hands pausing their movement. "Okay," he said, straightening but maintaining contact. "What I want to say about last night was that it was great and that I'd very much like for last night to happen again tonight."

The directness of his statement sent a flood of warmth through her body, pooling low in her abdomen. She turned, just enough to see his face.

"I'd like that too," she admitted. But even as desire kindled inside her, caution tempered the flame. She stepped away, needing physical space to think clearly. Her eyes met his, holding steady. "But I don't live in Galesburg."

His smile remained, but a seriousness entered his eyes. "I'm aware of that."

"I just don't want there to be any…confusion."

"You want to make sure I'm not going to get my heart broken." His voice was gentle, his expression open. He gave a shrug, his next words carrying a hint of resignation. "Unfortunately, I think it might be a little too late for that."

"Tyson—" she began, but he stepped forward and pressed a finger to her lips, the touch silencing her.

"I'm a big boy," he said, his finger moving from her lips to tuck a strand of hair behind her ear. "I know you have a life in DC and that you will have to go back to it at some point. But I like you. And I'm willing to see where this goes for as long as we have."

She studied his face, searching for any hint of deception or naivete, finding neither. Instead, she saw a man who had considered the odds and decided she was worth the risk. The realization caused something to shift inside her chest, a tender ache forming where moments before there had only been desire.

"Tyson…" she said again, his name both question and answer.

His expression lightened, a grin playing at the corners of his lips. "I really want to kiss you right now," he admitted, "but I don't know if I can make out in Amelia's house, so let's do what we came here to do and get out of here."

She recognized the deflection but decided not to push. Instead, she let a mischievous smile spread across her face. "So, you're saying you've never made out in Amelia's house. Good to know."

His laugh broke the tension.

They both turned their attention back to the photo album in her hands. She carefully flipped through the pages, each one a window into a past she'd never known. Images of Amelia and Annalise at a beach. At what appeared to be a high school dance, posing beside a vintage car. The sisters looked so young, so carefree.

"I'm not sure how an old photo album is going to help us," Tyson said, his voice close to her ear as he leaned in to see better.

She turned another page and immediately froze, her attention captured by a particular photograph. The breath caught in her throat as she studied it, her finger automatically moving to point at the image. "Isn't that Tom?"

He leaned closer, his chest now firmly against her back, his breath tickling her neck. Another shock of attraction rippled through her, but it was quickly overshadowed by the implications of what they were seeing.

"Yeah," he confirmed after a moment. "I think it's him. A few decades younger, but it's definitely him."

Her finger moved to the woman beside Tom. "But that's not Amelia. It's Annalise." Her mother's face, so similar to her own, stared back at her from the glossy surface of the photograph.

A heavy silence fell between them as they absorbed what they were seeing. In the photo, Tom and Annalise stood close together, caught in a moment of intimate laughter. Annalise's hand rested on Tom's jaw, turning his face toward hers for a kiss. Tom's arm circled Annalise's waist possessively, his other hand high on her thigh. The image captured a clear intimacy.

Tyson carefully removed the photo from its corner tabs, lifting it to examine it more closely. "They look cozy," he said, his voice neutral but thoughtful.

Her heartbeat thundered in her ears, her mind racing to connect dots she hadn't known existed until this moment. Tom and Annalise looked to be in their late teens in the photo.

Tyson watched her, waiting for her to process, to speak. She met his eyes, finding her voice at last. "You don't think? Could Tom be my birth father?"

"We don't know anything for certain yet," he reminded her gently. "This is just a photograph. It shows they knew each other, that they were...close." He paused, squeezing her hand. "But it doesn't prove he's your father."

"You're right. I'm getting ahead of myself." She took a deep breath, willing her racing thoughts to slow. "But it's a lead we didn't have before. A possibility."

He studied the photo again, his expression thoughtful. "Tom and Amelia have been friends for decades. I've known them both my whole life, and I never heard anything about him and

Annalise being together." He ran a hand over his hair. "But then, people don't always share everything, do they? Especially in small towns."

"No," she agreed, thinking of all the secrets her mother had kept. "They don't."

She carefully returned the photo to Tyson, who slipped it into his pocket rather than replacing it in the album. She returned the album to its place on the shelf, her fingers lingering on its spine for a moment before withdrawing.

"What now?" she asked, turning back to him.

His expression was resolute, his stance shifting subtly from lover to investigator. "Now I bring Tom in. See what he has to say." He paused, allowing the weight of the possibility to settle between them.

If their theory was correct that Waldo's murder and Amelia's attack had been perpetrated by her birth father in order to keep his identity secret, and if Tom was her birth father… She was getting ahead of herself again.

She met Tyson's gaze. "I need to know the truth," she said simply. "Whatever it is."

Tyson's arms came around her, pulling her against his chest. He pressed a kiss to the top of her head, his embrace solid and reassuring around her trembling form. "I know, sweetheart. And I promise you, we'll find out. We'll talk to Tom. Whatever the truth is, we'll uncover it together."

Chapter Twenty-Two

Tyson kept his car three lengths behind Olivia's as they wound through the quiet streets of Galesburg. The discovery at Amelia's house had left him unsettled. If Tom was Olivia's father, and if he'd been willing to kill Amelia, whom he supposedly loved, what wouldn't he do to keep Olivia from finding out the truth?

His chest tightened at the thought. He wouldn't let anything happen to her. Not now. Not when she was becoming someone he couldn't imagine losing.

They hadn't discussed him following her home. He'd simply fallen into place behind her at the intersection.

Tom and Annalise. The image from the photograph replayed in his mind—their bodies pressed together, their intimacy undeniable. If Tom was Olivia's father, it explained so much about Amelia's hostility, about the tension that had hung over their interactions from the beginning. But it also raised questions that made his detective's instincts buzz like live wires.

Olivia's brake lights flashed red as she slowed to turn onto the gravel drive leading to the lake house. He followed, the crunch of stones beneath his tires a counterpoint to his racing thoughts. The lake spread out before them, its surface gilded by the late afternoon sun. Under other circumstances, he might have paused to appreciate the view. Instead, his eyes swept the tree line, searching for anything out of place, any hint of movement that didn't belong.

Olivia parked in front of the house, and he pulled in beside her, angling his car to leave enough space between them. He was out of his vehicle before his engine fully quieted, scanning the surroundings one more time before focusing on Olivia as she emerged from her car. Her expression was distracted, preoccupied, no doubt by the same questions that plagued him. The wind lifted strands of her hair. She tucked them back with an absent gesture.

"I want to check inside before you go in," he called to her, his voice carrying easily in the still air. "Just to be safe."

She nodded, the tension in her shoulders visible even from where he stood. "Thank you."

He started toward her, covering the ground between their cars with long strides, already mentally going through the steps to clear the house. His mind so focused that he almost missed the subtle shift in the air that made the hair on the back of his neck stand up.

The crack of the gunshot split the silence.

He was moving before his mind fully registered what was happening, years of training taking over in an instant. "Get down!" he shouted, launching himself toward Olivia, who stood frozen in confusion, eyes wide as they darted around for the source of the sound.

He collided with her, one arm wrapping around her waist as he tackled her to the ground behind her car.

"Are you hit?" he asked Olivia, running his hands over her arms, her sides, checking for blood or injury.

"No," she managed to say, her voice tight with fear but steady enough to reassure him. "No, I'm okay."

More shots rang out, the bullets pinging against metal as they struck Olivia's car.

"Stay down," he ordered, his voice low and urgent against her ear as he covered her body with his own. Her breath came in panicked bursts against his neck. His own pulse thundered in his ears and adrenaline coursed through his body. He reached for his phone, keeping his body low, using the car for cover. He dialed dispatch, tucking the phone between his ear and shoulder while he drew his service weapon from the holster at his hip.

More shots came in rapid succession. He listened carefully, trying to pinpoint the direction they were coming from. From the west, maybe seventy yards away. It made sense based on what he knew of the rental property. The shooter would have the advantage of cover and elevation.

"This is Chief Morrow. Shots fired at 415 Lakeshore Drive. I've got an active shooter situation, at least one gunman in the woods west of the property. I need immediate backup." He rattled off additional details, their position, the approximate location of the shooter, the fact that they were pinned down with limited cover.

The dispatcher's voice came through, professional and calm. "Copy that, Chief. Units are en route."

The shooting had stopped. Tyson strained his ears, listening for movement, for any indication of what the shooter might be doing. Had they fled? Or was the shooter just repositioning?

"I think they're moving," he whispered to Olivia, who was pressed against him, her body trembling but her eyes clear and focused. "I need to go after them."

Her fingers dug into his arm. "Tyson—"

"I can't let them get away." He gently disentangled himself from her, making sure she was securely positioned behind the car's wheel well. "Stay here. Keep this line open." He handed her the phone. "Backup is on the way."

Before she could protest, he was moving, staying in a

crouch as he darted to the rear of the car. There was no gunfire, thankfully. He took a deep breath, then broke cover, sprinting for the tree line.

He hit the woods at full speed, immediately enveloped in the filtered green light beneath the canopy. The woods were dense, but ahead of him he could hear the sounds of someone else moving, branches breaking, leaves rustling, and the unmistakable cadence of running footsteps.

"Police! Stop!" he shouted.

The footsteps ahead of him speed up. He pushed himself harder, his lungs burning as he followed the sounds through the trees. He caught a glimpse of movement ahead. A dark figure ducked behind a large oak tree. He changed direction, hoping to intercept the shooter.

But the ground was full of roots and rocks and his foot caught, sending him stumbling to one knee. Pain shot up his leg, but he pushed back to his feet immediately. He could hear the shooter veering north, away from the lake, toward the county road that ran parallel to the shoreline, likely to a waiting vehicle.

He cursed under his breath and altered his course, crashing through a thicket of underbrush, branches scratching at his face and arms. He was losing ground. The shooter had too much of a head start and seemed to know these woods. By the time he reached the county road, it stretched empty in both directions, not a vehicle in sight. He turned in a slow circle, breathing hard, scanning for any sign of the shooter. Nothing. Whoever had shot at them was gone.

Damn it.

In the distance, he could hear sirens approaching, the backup he'd called for, too late. His right knee throbbed where he'd fallen, and a warm trickle of blood hit his cheek from a branch that had caught him during the chase.

He jogged back the way he'd come, moving more carefully now that the immediate danger appeared to have passed.

By the time he emerged from the trees, two patrol cars had arrived. Revis and Mingnala moved purposefully around the property, securing the scene, one of them speaking into a radio at the edge of the woods.

Olivia sat on the porch swing, her knees drawn up to her chest, arms wrapped around them. The sight of her, small and hunched in on herself, made his heart cinch. He crossed to her.

"Olivia," he said softly as he approached, not wanting to startle her.

She looked up, her face pale but composed, relief washing over her features as she recognized him. He sat beside her, wincing as his injured knee protested the movement.

"You're bleeding," she said, reaching up to touch his cheek. Her fingers came away red.

"It's nothing. Just a scratch." He took her hand in his, squeezing it gently. "Are you okay?"

She nodded, but the tremor in her fingers belied her outward calm. "Did you find them?"

He shook his head, frustration creasing his brow. "No. They knew these woods too well and had an escape route planned. They were gone by the time I reached the road."

"Someone just tried to kill us," Olivia said, the reality of it seeming to hit her anew. Her voice shook, anger threading through the fear.

"I know." He wrapped her in his arms. "I will find out who it was."

She searched his face. "Do you think…" She hesitated, then pushed forward. "Do you think it was Tom?"

"I don't know," he said honestly. "I only caught a glimpse of the person." He plucked pine needles and bits of leaves from his hair. "But the way they navigated those woods, how quickly they disappeared..." He let the thought trail off.

"Tom grew up in Galesburg," Olivia finished for him. "He would know these woods very well."

He nodded slowly. "Yes. He would." He'd known Tom his entire life, and the idea that he could be behind this, that he could have shot at them with the intent to kill, was hard to process.

He could hear the officers calling to each other as they began to search the perimeter, looking for shell casings and other evidence. Soon this quiet lakeside would be transformed into a full crime scene, techs combing every inch, photographers documenting everything.

"As soon as I know you're safe," he said, his voice hardening with resolve, "I'm going to find out exactly where Tom was five minutes ago."

Chapter Twenty-Three

Tyson watched Tom through the one-way glass, studying the man he'd known all his life as he sat alone at the metal table. Tom's fingers drummed an irregular rhythm on the scratched surface, his shoulders hunched beneath his flannel shirt. The harsh fluorescent lights cast shadows on Tom's face, deepening the lines around his mouth, making him look older than he was. Olivia stood beside Tyson, her eyes fixed on the man who might be her father.

"I need to go in there," he said, his voice low. "Are you sure you want to watch this?"

Olivia nodded without looking at him, her gaze still locked on Tom. "I need to hear what he has to say."

He studied her profile. The fatigue etched around her eyes, shadows that hadn't been there when they'd first met. The urge to protect her swelled in his chest, but he knew better. Olivia wouldn't leave without whatever answers Tom could provide.

"Okay. But remember," he said, touching her elbow gently, "whatever happens in there, whatever he says...we're still just gathering information."

The warning was as much for himself as for her. He couldn't afford to let his personal feelings cloud his judgment. Not his concern for Olivia or his lifelong respect for Tom. The facts would lead where they would, regardless of what either of them wanted them to be.

He took a deep breath, letting it out slowly before he left the observation room and went into the interrogation room where Tom waited.

Tom looked up, relief washing over his features at the sight of a familiar face. “Tyson. Finally.” Tom attempted a smile that didn’t reach his eyes. “What’s going on? Your message sounded urgent.”

Tyson pulled out the chair opposite Tom and sat down, placing the folder in his hands on the table between them. “Thanks for coming in, Tom. I appreciate your cooperation.” He kept his tone professional but not cold. “We’ve uncovered some new information in Amelia’s case, and I needed to ask you a few questions.”

Tom’s shoulders relaxed. “Of course. Anything that helps find who hurt Amelia.”

Tyson nodded, maintaining eye contact as he began with routine questions, confirming Tom’s full name, address, his relationship to Amelia.

“How long have you known Amelia?” he asked.

“All my life, basically. Our families were neighbors. We grew up together.” Tom’s expression softened with genuine affection. “She’s one of my oldest friends.”

He made a note in the file, buying himself a moment to transition to more difficult territory. “And her sister, Annalise. Did you know her well?”

Something flickered across Tom’s face, so briefly Tyson might have missed it if he hadn’t been watching closely.

“Annalise? Not really. I knew her, of course. She was Amelia’s sister. But we weren’t close.” Tom’s eyes dropped to his hands before coming back up to meet Tyson’s gaze. “Why? What does Annalise have to do with what happened to Amelia?”

A lie.

"When was the last time you saw Annalise?" Tyson pressed, ignoring Tom's question.

Tom's brow furrowed. "I don't know. Must have been before she left town. Thirty, thirty-five years ago? Like I said, we weren't close."

Tyson leaned forward, resting his forearms on the table. "Tom, I've known you my whole life. I've always respected you. So, I'm going to be direct here." He paused, gauging Tom's reaction. "We have reason to believe that you and Annalise were more than just acquaintances."

Tom's face remained carefully blank, but his knuckles whitened as he clasped his hands together on the table. "I don't know what you're talking about."

"I think you do." Tyson reached into the folder and withdrew the photograph they'd found at Amelia's house. He placed it on the table, sliding it toward Tom. "That's you and Annalise, isn't it?"

Tom stared at the photograph, the color draining from his face. Tyson watched the older man closely, cataloging first shock, then recognition and finally resignation. He wondered what Olivia was thinking behind the mirror but was careful not to look that way and let Tom know someone was watching.

"Where did you get this?" Tom's voice had grown more defensive.

"I found it at Amelia's house." Tyson kept his tone even. "I was looking for anything that might help us understand who would want to hurt her."

Tom ran a hand over his face, looking every one of his years. The silence stretched between them, heavy with unspoken history.

"Yes," he admitted. "That's me and Annalise."

"So, you were involved with her." Tyson stated it as a fact, not a question.

Tom sighed, his shoulders slumping. "It wasn't serious. We dated for a little while, that's all. It was—" he gestured vaguely, searching for words "—puppy love, I guess you'd call it. More on my part than hers."

"When was this?"

"Spring of '95. A few weeks, that's all the relationship amounted to." Tom's gaze returned to the photograph, something like nostalgia softening his expression. "I was crazy about her. But Annalise…she was always looking beyond Galesburg. I was just a pit stop for her."

He mentally compared the timeline to what they knew. "Olivia was born in December 1995."

Tom's head snapped up, his eyes narrowing. "What are you getting at, Tyson?"

"I think you know." Tyson held his gaze steadily. "Annalise left town pregnant. The timing fits."

"No." Tom shook his head emphatically. "No, that's not possible. Olivia couldn't be mine."

"You seem very certain of that."

"I am certain." Tom leaned forward. "Annalise and I, we never—" He broke off, uncomfortable. "Look, we fooled around, sure, but we were never intimate."

He raised an eyebrow, skeptical. If Tom was telling the truth, he and Annalise were dating at the same time that Annalise was seeing the father of her baby.

"I was raised Catholic," Tom continued. "And Annalise, well, she had her own reasons for not wanting to sleep with me." He sighed. "Look, believe what you want, but I couldn't be Olivia's father."

"Why did you lie about dating Annalise in the first place?"

Tom's gaze dropped to the table, his shoulders slumped. "Because Amelia doesn't know." At Tyson's surprised expression, he continued, "At least I thought she didn't know. By the time Amelia and I started dating, so much time had passed it was ancient history."

He considered this, turning it over in his mind. It was plausible. People kept stranger secrets for less convincing reasons, but something still felt off.

"Tom, someone shot at Olivia and me earlier today at the lake house." He watched closely for any reaction. "We think it might be connected to what happened to Amelia. Where were you between noon and five?"

Tom's eyes widened, genuine shock registering on his face. "Someone shot at you? Jesus, Tyson." He shook his head. "I was at The Grill from about twelve thirty until a little after two. I had a business lunch with a supplier. There were at least a dozen people who can vouch for me."

He nodded, making a note to check the alibi, though Tom's reaction seemed authentic. "And the night Amelia was attacked?"

"I've already spoken with your Officer Revis. I was home, alone." Tom's expression darkened. "I know that's not an alibi, but I didn't hurt Amelia. I wouldn't. I love her."

He weighed everything he'd heard against everything he knew about Tom. The man sitting across from him was the same person who'd shown up at his mother's house with a casserole and quiet support after her funeral. Could he really have shot at him and Olivia? Could he have attacked Amelia?

His gut said no. But his training reminded him that people were complex, capable of compartmentalizing. Of justifying the most heinous acts.

"Is there anything else you can tell me that might help us figure out who's behind these attacks?"

Tom spread his hands, helplessness written in the gesture. "I wish there was. I've been wracking my brain since Amelia was hurt, trying to think if she mentioned any threats, any problems. But there was nothing out of the ordinary."

He nodded, gathering his notes. "Alright. Wait here for a few minutes. I need to check on something, then I'll be back."

He left the interrogation room, closing the door firmly behind him. In the hallway, he paused, exhaling slowly, letting the tension ease from his shoulders. If Tom was telling the truth, and Tyson believed he was, then they were back to square one with regards to the murder and assault cases and Olivia's paternity.

He entered the observation room to find Olivia still standing close to the glass, her arms wrapped around herself as if for protection. She looked at him, her expression a mix of emotions he couldn't decipher.

"What do you think?" he asked, moving to stand beside her.

Her gaze returned to Tom, who sat slumped at the table, looking weary and defeated. "I don't know. Part of me believes him when he says he's not my father, but…"

"But?"

"But I see things." She gestured toward Tom. "The shape of his hands. The way he tilts his head when he's thinking. They're familiar." She turned to him, vulnerability in her eyes. "Is that just my imagination? Am I seeing what I want to see?"

He wished he had a definitive answer for her. "I believe he's telling the truth about his relationship with your mother. He also wasn't married at the time of his relationship with your mother and that doesn't fit with the man Sarah Garrett told us about."

She sighed, rubbing her temples. "I don't know. Nothing about this makes sense." She straightened suddenly, resolve hardening her features. "I want to talk to him."

"Olivia—"

"Just one question. That's all I need to ask."

"Alright," he said, relenting. "But I have to stay in the room with you. And if he doesn't want to talk, I can make him."

"Fine." She nodded, moving toward the door.

He followed, a protective instinct keeping him close as they walked down the hallway to the interrogation room. He opened the door for her. Tom's head snapped up, surprise on his face at seeing Olivia enter behind him.

"Olivia?" Confusion colored Tom's voice. "What are you doing here?"

Olivia sat in the chair Tyson had vacated, her back straight. "I have a question for you," she said, her voice steady despite a slight tremor in her hands. "Are you my birth father?"

The directness of the question seemed to catch Tom off guard. He blinked, then shook his head slowly. "No, Olivia. I'm not. I couldn't be, for the reasons I explained to Tyson."

"You're certain?" Olivia held his gaze, seemingly searching for any sign of deception.

"I am." Tom's voice was gentle but firm. "I understand why you're asking, and why this matters to you. But I am not your father."

A long moment of silence stretched between them, filled with the weight of paths not taken, lives that might have been lived differently. Olivia nodded, acceptance—if not full belief—in the gesture.

"Would you be willing to take a DNA test?" she asked.

Tom didn't hesitate. "Of course. Whatever you need."

"Thank you." Olivia stood, the single motion graceful despite the emotional weight she carried. "That's all I wanted to know."

Tyson pushed away from the wall, moving to open the door for her. "We'll be in touch about the test," he told Tom. "You're free to go for now, but stay available. We might have more questions."

Tom nodded, rising from his chair. "I understand. And, Tyson?" He paused at the doorway. "Find who did this. Find who hurt Amelia."

"I will," he promised.

He let Tom leave then led Olivia back to his office, aware of the curious glances from other officers as they passed.

His office door closed behind them with a satisfying click and she sank into one of the visitors' chairs. She looked exhausted.

"You should get some rest," Tyson said, concern overriding everything else. "This has been—"

"Overwhelming?" she suggested with a weak smile.

"That's one word for it." Tyson moved around his desk, resisting the urge to pull her into his arms. The glass walls of his office made them visible to the entire bullpen, and he was acutely aware of maintaining professional boundaries while on duty. Still, he crouched in front of her and took her hands in his.

"I need to stay here, check Tom's alibi, follow up on a few leads," he said, hating the idea of sending her away but knowing it was necessary. "But I don't want you alone at the lake house, not after what happened."

She nodded. "What do you suggest?"

"I'll have an officer take you there and remain outside." He reached for the phone on his desk. "And I'll come by as soon as I can. A few hours, tops."

"You don't have to—"

"I want to," he interrupted, the intensity in his voice surprising them both. He softened his tone. "I'll feel better knowing you're safe. And we can talk more then, figure out our next steps."

She studied him for a long moment, something unreadable in her gaze. Finally, she nodded. "Okay. A few hours."

As he arranged for a patrol car to take Olivia home and an officer to stand guard, he watched her gather her strength, pulling herself together with visible effort. She was resilient, and was already someone he couldn't imagine losing. The thought sent a chill through him. What if the shooter tried again? What if next time they succeeded?

Ten minutes later, Tyson stood in the parking lot, watching until the police cruiser disappeared around the corner. He squared his shoulders and turned back toward the station, his mind shifting to the tasks ahead.

Someone had tried to kill Olivia. Had put Amelia in the hospital. Had murdered Waldo Emerson. Someone was willing to go to great lengths to keep their secrets buried. He had to uncover those secrets.

He pulled out his phone as he walked, dialing the hospital. Amelia's condition hadn't changed, but he left word to call immediately if she woke up. If only she would wake up, she might be able to tell them who'd hurt her and put an end to all of this. Until then, all he had were questions, suspicions and a growing fear that time was running out.

Chapter Twenty-Four

Olivia paced the length of the lake house living room, the wooden floorboards creaking beneath her steps. Outside, the radio of the police cruiser Tyson had stationed at her rental punctuated the evening quiet. It was a reminder that she wasn't completely alone, but it was of little comfort. It was also a reminder that Tyson thought someone wanted her dead.

It had been hours since she'd left Tyson at the station and she was anxious to see him again, to make sure he was okay and because she never felt safer than when he was near. What was taking him so long? Her fingers itched to call him, but she knew he needed to work without her interruptions. The waiting was torture.

She paused at the window, peering out at the silhouette of the young officer in the patrol car. He sat motionless, his attention fixed out the windshield on something Olivia couldn't see.

She moved to the kitchen to make herself a cup of tea. The familiar ritual, filling the kettle, selecting a bag from the canister, gave her something to think about other than her current situation. But not for long. Her mind circled around Tom's denial that she was his daughter, Waldo Emerson's death and Amelia's attack. If Tom wasn't her father, who was? And was that man behind Amelia's assault? And was Amelia's assault really connected to Waldo's murder? She understood Tyson's hesitance to believe these events were just coincidences, but there was no real evidence they were connected either. It was all so frustrating. Every time she thought she was close to getting answers, she found herself with more questions.

The tea kettle whistled. She picked it up with one hand and turned off the burner with the other. A gentle scraping sounded at the back of the house. Olivia froze, kettle suspended above the sink. Had she imagined it? The house settled again into silence, and she exhaled slowly.

"Old houses make noises," she said out loud, reassuring herself as she poured the hot water into a mug.

The second sound was unmistakable. A soft thud followed by the distinct creak of a floorboard. That was no settling house. Her heart lurched against her ribs. Someone was inside the house.

She set the tea kettle down with trembling hands, careful not to make a sound. Her phone was in the living room, too far to reach without crossing open space, but the kitchen was full of weapons. She grabbed a large knife from the knife block on the counter just as another creak sounded. This one was closer, seeming to have come from the hallway leading from the front of the house.

She had to get to the officer outside.

She moved toward the back door, as quickly as she could and still trying not to let the intruder know she knew they were there. The wood floors she'd so admired seemed determined to betray her. Each step seemed to send a thundering creak through the house as she padded forward. She reached the back door and eased it open just enough to slip through.

The night air hit her face, cool and damp with lake mist. She hurried down the rear porch steps and ran around the side of her house toward the patrol car. She realized something was wrong before she made it all the way to the vehicle. She eased forward. "Officer Mingnala?" she called, her voice barely above a whisper. "Officer Mingnala, someone's in the house."

There was no response. The officer remained completely motionless.

She moved closer to the car, dread pooling in her stomach. As she drew nearer, she could see blood streaking the window on the driver's-side window. She yanked the car door open.

The young officer groaned, stirring. He was alive, but his breathing was shallow and labored. The front of the police radio was shattered, the wires exposed.

"Oh God," Olivia whispered, reaching for him.

She needed her phone, but it was inside with the intruder. Officer Mingnala probably had a cell phone, but a quick scan of the car didn't reveal it, and she wasn't sure she should move him trying to find it. She hesitated, unsure what to do. She could run, try to make her way through the woods to the nearest house. Or she could take her chances going back inside to get her phone.

The officer's eyes fluttered open, glazed with pain, his voice barely audible. "Help."

She couldn't leave the officer. He didn't have time for her to bumble through the woods. She needed to get her phone and call for help. It would take less than a minute if she moved fast.

Olivia turned back toward the house, knife still clutched in her hand. She had taken three steps when a figure emerged from the shadows beside the front porch. She recognized the man immediately, although his presence made no sense.

"Marcus?" Her voice faltered, confusion momentarily overriding her fear.

Marcus Santini stood before her, his lined face grave in the dim light.

"Olivia," he said, his voice oddly gentle. "I need you to come with me. Now."

He gestured toward the house, his manner calm but insistent. In his other hand, she glimpsed something that made her blood run cold, a gun, held low but pointed directly at her.

"You shot him," she said, the realization hitting her. "You shot the officer."

Marcus's expression remained unchanged. "Please don't make this more difficult than it has to be."

She tightened her grip on the knife, calculating her chances of reaching the road before he could stop her. As if reading her thoughts, Marcus raised the gun.

"I don't want to hurt you, Olivia," he said. "But I will if I have to. Now drop the knife and let's go to the dock."

She had no choice. She let the knife slide from her hand and, with Marcus following close behind, she walked around the side of the house to the dock. The lake stretched beyond the backyard, dark water lapping gently at the private dock where a motorboat was tethered beside the one belonging to the rental house.

"Get in," he ordered, gesturing toward the boat.

"Why are you doing this?" she demanded, turning to face him. "What do you want?"

A flicker of emotion that she couldn't place passed across his face before Marcus wiped it away. "I didn't want any of this to happen. I had a good life, a reputation in this town. But then you came, asking questions, digging up the past." Marcus studied her face for a long moment. "You have her eyes. Annalise's eyes."

The implication of his words sent a cold wave through her body. "What are you saying? Are you…are you my father?"

Marcus stilled and was silent for so long, she wasn't sure she would answer. "Annalise and I had an affair. I was older, married, building my career with an eye on a judgeship. A baby out of wedlock would have ruined everything."

She stared at him, disbelief warring with a horrible sense of recognition.

"Annalise agreed to put you up for adoption," he continued, his voice soft now. "She was young, but she understood she couldn't raise a child. I arranged everything through a lawyer friend, Waldo Sr. Everything was done. But then Annalise changed her mind."

"After I was born?" she whispered.

"A few months after. She wanted to know where you were. She wanted to get you back." His mouth twisted into a scowl. "I couldn't allow that."

The pieces fell into place with sickening clarity. "You killed her. You killed Annalise."

He didn't deny it. "Everything would have stayed buried if you hadn't come to town and started asking questions. Waldo Jr. tried to blackmail me. His father been taking payments for years to keep quiet, and I thought it was over when he died but then you came to town and Waldo thought he could pick up where his father left off. And Amelia—" He shook his head. "I wasn't sure what she knew about Annalise and me. I couldn't risk it."

"You attacked Amelia?" Horror rose in her throat like bile. "She was your friend."

"I'm too old to let my legacy be tarnished now," he said, as if that excused everything he'd done. "I can't let Geo or anyone else in town know."

"Even if keeping your secret means killing your own daughter?" she asked, her voice breaking despite her effort to remain strong. She stared at the man in front of her, her biological father, and saw nothing of herself reflected back, no warmth, no recognition of their shared blood at all. She was merely a problem to be solved, an inconvenience to be eliminated.

"I'm sorry," he said.

The boat rocked beneath his feet as Marcus forced her onto it, his gun pressing into the small of her back. The lake's surface rippled darkly around them. She stumbled onto the deck of the boat, her mind racing for a way out.

Marcus kept the gun trained on her as he untied the mooring line with one hand. She was unarmed, outmatched and running out of time.

"Sit down," he ordered, gesturing with the gun to a bench seat.

My father, she thought, the words bitter as poison. This stranger who had helped create her, who had killed her mother, who'd thought of her as an inconvenient piece of evidence. Who still thought of her that way. His rejection cut deeper than she would have thought possible. Even though she'd known he hadn't wanted her, a part of her had held on to the fantasy that he was a good man who simply had to make a difficult decision. That he'd welcome her into his life once he knew who she was. The reality of her current situation mocked those childish dreams.

Marcus started the boat's engine, its low rumble shattering the night's quiet. The boat edged away from the dock, water slapping against its hull.

"You don't have to do this," she said, fighting to keep her voice steady. "No one knows what you've told me. We could go back, forget this happened."

A humorless smile twisted his mouth. "You're not a very convincing liar."

He was right. Even as the words had left her mouth, they'd rung false. She would never forget, never stop seeking justice for her mother and they both knew it.

The boat picked up speed, cutting through the water, putting more distance between them and the shore with each passing second. Soon they would be in the deepest part of the lake, where the cold water could easily swallow a body. Her mind flashed to Tyson, probably still at the station, unaware of her danger. Would he find her? Would he piece together what had happened? Or would she simply become a mysterious disappearance, another unsolved case?

No. The word formed in her mind with fierce clarity. She would not die without a fight. She would not let this man get away with another murder.

She watched him, calculating. Marcus was in his sixties, but still fit, still strong. The gun gave him an obvious advantage, but he needed to steer the boat, which occupied one hand. If she could somehow get him off balance…

"Did you ever think about me?" she asked, the question genuine despite its strategic purpose. "Over the years, did you ever wonder what happened to your daughter?"

Marcus's eyes flicked to her face, then back to the water ahead. "I made my choice a long time ago."

"That's not an answer." She shifted her weight, readying to spring as the boat rocked beneath them.

"What do you want me to say?" Irritation edged his voice. "That I regretted it? That I kept track of you? I didn't. You were a problem that was solved."

The casual cruelty of his words stoked an anger hot and fierce in her chest. She lunged forward, aiming for the hand that held the gun. Marcus reacted with surprising speed, swinging the weapon toward her, but her momentum carried her into his midsection before he could get off a shot. They collided, the impact sending them both staggering backward.

The boat lurched wildly, rocking dangerously with no one at the helm. She grabbed for the gun, her fingers closing around his wrist, twisting with all her strength. He grunted in pain but maintained his grip, using his greater weight to force her backward until her spine pressed against the boat's edge.

"Stop fighting," he hissed, face inches from hers. "You'll only make it worse for yourself."

Her answer was a sharp upward jerk of her knee, aiming for his groin. Marcus twisted, avoiding the worst of the blow, but the movement loosened his grip on her. She wrenched herself sideways, putting precious inches between them. The boat pitched again, sending a spray of cold water over the side that stung her face.

He recovered quickly, lunging for her with the gun raised like a club. She dodged, but the confined space of the boat left her nowhere to go. The blow caught her shoulder instead of her head, pain exploding down her arm. Her feet tangled with a coiled rope on the deck and she stumbled.

"I didn't want this," Marcus said, advancing on her again. "If you'd just stayed away."

She scrambled backward, her injured arm throbbing. The boat's edge pressed against her back once more, the dark water lapping hungrily just inches below. His face loomed above her, half in shadows. His hand closed around her throat, pushing her farther back over the edge of the boat. She fought, clawing at his arm, but she was weakening. Her mind cut to thoughts of Amelia, still unconscious in her hospital bed, and the relationship they'd never have. And Stephanie's easy acceptance. And Tyson. The thought of him sent a wave of sorrow through her. What might they have become to each other, given time?

Her vision began to darken at the edges, her lungs burning for air. With one last desperate burst of strength, she pushed him at the same time the boat lurched. He lost his grip on her, but her weight was unbalanced. Another sudden lurch of the boat and Olivia was falling, the lake water rising to meet her. Water closed over her head, swallowing her.

Chapter Twenty-Five

Tyson's knuckles blanched white as he took the curve too fast, tires screaming on asphalt. Officer Mingnala's radio check-ins had stopped abruptly a half hour ago. He'd tried Olivia's phone a half dozen times and gotten no response. Each unanswered call had ratcheted his anxiety higher, until the dread was a cold weight pressing against his lungs. The rational part of his mind tried to conjure innocent explanations. Cell phone service was spotty by the lake. Olivia might be in the shower. Mingnala could have stepped away from his radio momentarily. But every nerve in his body screamed that Olivia was in danger.

Officer Mingnala wouldn't have gone radio silent unless something was terribly wrong. The kid was meticulous and reliable to a fault. And Olivia would have never ignored his calls. After everything they'd discovered, she wouldn't have left him to worry.

The lake house finally appeared around the bend, its windows dark against the night sky. He cut his headlights as he approached and coasted the last hundred yards up the gravel drive.

The patrol car sat where it should be, but even in the moonlight, Tyson could see that something was wrong. The driver's-side window reflected odd patterns, the glass fractured in a way that sent ice through his veins. He pulled up behind it, killed his engine and drew his weapon before getting out of the car.

"Mingnala," he called, approaching the car with his gun held ready.

The unmistakable copper tang of blood hit him first. Then he saw Officer Mingnala slumped against the door. Blood matted the young man's hair, streaked his uniform, pooled darkly on the seat beneath him.

Tyson whispered a swear word, yanking the door open.

Mingnala's eyes fluttered at the movement, a groan escaping his lips. Relief flooded him, immediately tempered by the severity of the man's wounds. "Hang on. I'm going to get you help." He drew his cell phone out of his pocket and called for an ambulance, his eyes continuously scanning for threats as he did. The call took seconds, but each moment was like hours wondering where Olivia was. Once the ambulance was on the way, he turned his focus back to Mingnala.

"What happened? Where's Olivia?"

The wounded officer's lips moved, but the words were too faint to hear. He leaned closer, his ear almost touching Officer Mingnala's mouth.

"Marcus Santini," Mingnala managed to say, his words barely a breath. "Took her. Boat."

Tyson's head snapped up, his gaze going to the lake stretching behind the house. Marcus? Marcus Santini? The thought seemed impossible. Marcus was a local judge and a pillar of the community. He was friends with Amelia. Yet even as his mind struggled to process this new information, the pieces were starting to fit.

A flash of light out on the water caught his attention. Squinting, he made out the silhouette of a boat moving across the water with two figures on it.

Olivia.

He was running before he made the conscious decision to move. There was only one thought in his head. Getting to Olivia.

Another boat rocked beside the dock. He leaped aboard. The keys weren't in the ignition. Of course not. People didn't leave keys in boats, not even in Galesburg. His eyes swept the deck of the boat for storage compartments or anywhere else a key could be kept. Nothing.

Damn it. He scanned the water and saw that the other boat was getting farther and farther away. Almost frantic now, he returned to searching the boat, sliding his hand beneath the seat. His fingers connected with cold metal. A magnetic key holder. Thank God for small town habits.

The engine coughed then roared to life. He pushed the throttle forward, sending the boat surging over the dark water. Wind whipped at his face, but he pushed the boat faster, closing the distance between himself and the other boat.

He could make out details of the people on the other boat now. Marcus stood over Olivia with his hands around her throat. Olivia appeared to weaken. Her body arched backward, and then she disappeared over the side of the boat.

"No!" The scream tore from his throat. Marcus scrambled for something on the deck. A gun, Tyson realized when the older man stood and aimed the weapon at the water that Olivia had fallen into.

He's going to shoot her when she surfaces.

The distance between the two boats closed with excruciating slowness, but there was no more time.

Tyson raised his weapon, bracing himself against the boat's rocking motion, doing his best to steady his aim. "Marcus!" he shouted. "Drop the gun!"

Whether Marcus couldn't hear over the engines or simply didn't care, he couldn't tell. The man remained focused on the water, his own gun trained downward, waiting for Olivia to resurface. The boats were close enough now that Tyson could now see Marcus's face. His features were set with a terrible determination that left no room for mercy.

Olivia was going to die if he didn't act now. He steadied his breathing and squeezed the trigger.

The shot was deafening in the night quiet. Marcus jerked as the bullet struck him. His body twisted 180 degrees and then seemed to freeze for a moment. Marcus's eyes met his as the boats came side to side, a look of surprise replacing the determination that he had previously seen on the judge's face. Then Marcus toppled sideways, disappearing into the lake with a splash.

Tyson cut his boat's engine, the sudden silence ringing in his ears. His eyes searched the dark water frantically, seeking any sign of Olivia. "Olivia! Olivia!"

A disturbance in the water caught his attention, ripples spread outward about twenty feet from the boat. He didn't hesitate before stripping off his shoes and diving into the lake.

The cold water hit him, shocking the air from his lungs. Beneath the water's surface everything was black. He kicked downward, arms outstretched, blindly searching for her.

His lungs burned, demanding air, but he swam deeper. His fingers brushed fabric, and he grasped it desperately, pulling the weight toward him. Olivia's face materialized from the darkness, her hair floating around her features like seaweed, her eyes closed. He wrapped his arm around her chest and kicked for the surface as if his life depended on it.

He broke the surface with Olivia still terrifyingly still in his grip. He swam one-armed to the nearer boat and pulled her onto it with strength that could only be attributed to the rush of adrenaline surging through his body.

Her skin had a bluish cast, her lips colorless.

No, no, no.

He began doing CPR and silently begging God, fate and whoever else might be listening to help him. Olivia's body convulsed suddenly, water spewing from her mouth as she began to cough violently. Relief swept through him with such force that his vision blurred.

"That's it," he said encouragingly, helping her sit up as she continued to expel water. "You're okay. I've got you."

Her coughing subsided, replaced by deep, shuddering breaths. Her eyes found his in the darkness, recognition and relief flooding her features. "Tyson," she managed to say, her voice raw.

The sound of his name on her lips undid something in him. He pulled her against his chest, arms encircling her with fierce protectiveness. She was alive.

"I thought I'd lost you," he whispered into her hair. "God, Olivia, I thought—"

Her body trembled against his, violent shudders that had as much to do with shock as with the cold water. He pulled back just enough to see her face, to assure himself again that she was really here, really safe. Her skin was ice beneath his fingers as he brushed wet hair from her forehead.

"It was Marcus," she said, her teeth chattering. "It was all Marcus. He's my father and he tried to kill me."

The words were almost as chilling as the water. Marcus was Olivia's father. The man he'd known all his life. The man he'd just shot. The implications swirled in his mind, but he pushed them aside. Later. There would be time to untangle all of it later.

"Don't worry. He can't hurt you now," he said, pulling her close again. "It's over. You're safe."

Her fingers curled into his soaked shirt, clinging to him as if she might drift away without this anchor. "He killed my mother," she whispered against his chest. "He was going to kill me too."

He tightened his hold on her, one hand cradling the back of her head. The woman in his arms had come into his life like a sudden storm, and now he couldn't imagine a world without her in it. "I'm sorry," he said. "I'm so sorry I didn't get here sooner."

She pulled back, her eyes finding his in the darkness. "You saved my life."

"I will always come for you," he promised, the words feeling like a vow more binding than any he'd made before.

She lifted her hand to his face, fingers tracing his cheek with tender exploration. The touch undid him. He leaned forward and pressed his lips to hers. The kiss was gentle, reverent, a confirmation of life and possibility.

When they parted, he rested his forehead against hers, breathing her in. "It's all going to be okay," he whispered, willing it to be true. "We'll figure everything out. Together."

In the distance, sirens wailed. Backup finally. The truth would be pieced together, the full story of betrayal and secrets spanning decades revealed. But in that moment there was only Olivia alive in his arms, and that was more than enough for now.

Chapter Twenty-Six

Olivia's heart pounded as she watched Tyson step into Amelia's Café. She had spotted him before he noticed her with Stephanie, Amelia, Hanes, Geo and the crowd of regular patrons gathered for the little celebration marking Amelia's first day back at work. Tyson scanned the room, his gaze finally landing on her, and a smile spread across his face.

He headed toward Amelia first, wrapping her in a warm embrace, then moved to hug Stephanie, but his eyes kept darting in Olivia's direction. She couldn't help but admire how handsome he looked in his jeans and white button-down shirt, his badge displayed on his hip.

It had been three weeks since Marcus had tried to kill her. He hadn't survived his gunshot wound, and while she didn't take pleasure in his death, she hoped that wherever he was, he was paying for the lives he had taken. At least she, Amelia and Stephanie now knew the truth about what had happened to Annalise. She hoped her mother could finally rest in peace.

Amelia laughed and Olivia marveled at how quickly her aunt had recovered. She had awakened from her coma just a day after the kidnapping, and although she was still recovering, her resilience was nothing short of remarkable. It had been harder for Stephanie and Geo to work through the fact that Geo's father had caused so much hurt to so many people Stephanie loved—including Geo, who was conflicted about what his father had done and overwhelmed at learning Olivia was his half sister—but they were committed to getting through it.

And they weren't the only couple, tending to a fledgling relationship. Olivia had returned to DC but she and Tyson spoke every day. The late-night phone conversations with Tyson over the past three weeks had been a lifeline for her. Her excitement about actually seeing him again had been growing for days.

And now here he was. The sight of him made her pulse quicken. She hoped he would be as excited about the decision she had made as she was.

Finally free from Amelia's and Stephanie's attention, Tyson made his way to Olivia, a drink in hand. He stood close enough that she could smell his cologne, the familiar scent sending another flutter through her stomach.

"It's so good to see you," he said, his voice low. "You look beautiful."

The compliment spread warmth through her entire body, a blush rising to her cheeks. "I'm happy to see you too," she replied. "You look very handsome."

He rubbed one hand over the front of his shirt and preened. "Well, I may have put in a little extra effort today for somebody special," he said with a wink.

She grinned. "Well, I have a surprise for you too."

"Oh?" Tyson's eyebrows raised in curiosity.

"Amelia has asked me to redesign her logo, menus, napkins. All the café's marketing materials."

"That's great. Congratulations," he said, genuine happiness in his tone.

"There's only one catch," she continued. "The contract requires me to work from Galesburg until the job is done."

A huge grin spread across Tyson's face. "Oh, really?" He set his drink down and slid a hand around her waist.

"Really," she confirmed, wrapping her arms around him

and shooting a quick glance over her shoulder at Amelia. "And something tells me my aunt is going to be a very demanding client that keeps me busy."

Tyson leaned down until his lips touched hers lightly. "I sure hope so."

* * * * *